MORE DANGEROUS THAN MAN

A TANNER NOVEL - BOOK 10

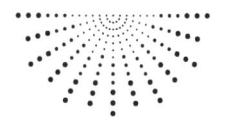

REMINGTON KANE

YEAR ZERO

INTRODUCTION

MORE DANGEROUS THAN MAN – A TANNER NOVEL – BOOK 10

Tanner makes his way across the country to see an old friend as he seeks answers about his past.

Meanwhile, female assassin Alexa Lucia is searching for Tanner. But is she an ally or an enemy?

ACKNOWLEDGMENTS

I write for you.

—Remington Kane

1
SURPRISE!

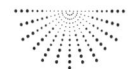

OKLAHOMA CITY, OKLAHOMA

Tanner realized he was being followed after he left the drive-thru lane of a fast food restaurant.

One of the cars in line behind him pulled out without getting their food. The unusual behavior caught Tanner's attention.

Whoever was driving wasn't a complete idiot, because he allowed several cars to come between them, so that he wasn't driving directly behind Tanner. There were two men in the car. From the brief glimpse Tanner got of them as they passed beneath a street light, they appeared to be about his age. They were likely just two more punks looking to cash in on the million-dollar bounty that Alonso Alvarado had placed on his head.

Tanner drove in a pattern that left no doubt he was being followed, then he headed straight for his motel. When he got there, he parked in front of his room, Room 4, and entered just as the two men parked several spaces away. He made certain to look in their direction, so that they could get a good look at him.

If they thought they had made a mistake and followed the wrong man they might leave. Tanner didn't want them to leave because he needed information.

~

THE TWO MEN FOLLOWING TANNER WERE NAMED DERRICK and Bobby. They were locals, and Bobby had spotted Tanner while stopped at a traffic light.

Derrick was the more aggressive of the two and a former boxer. His nose and ears spoke of his losses in the ring, but he retained the good looks he was born with.

Bobby was a follower, skinny as a reed, and had thinning blond hair. He had been a fair basketball player in high school, but when he failed to get a college scholarship, he joined the army. That's where he and Derrick met.

After parking in the motel lot, Derrick took another look at the drawing of Tanner's face.

"Yeah, I wasn't sure until he looked this way, but there can't be two guys with eyes like his."

Bobby checked to see if his gun was loaded for the third time since spotting Tanner. While he did that, Derrick pumped a shell into his shotgun and told Bobby how they would do it.

"You go around back and make sure he doesn't sneak out, I think the bathrooms here have a small window in them."

"You've stayed here?"

Derrick smiled as he cut off the car's engine. "That waitress at Elmo's Bar, you know the one with the long legs? I nailed her here about a year ago."

"Get out of here! You slept with Mindy?"

"Yeah, but just once, she said it was her way of paying her husband back for something or other."

"Damn Derrick, that girl is hot."

"Yeah, but she sucked in bed. Never mind that, you go head around back, wait a full minute, and then you'll hear me kick in the door. If this Tanner dude tries to leave through the bathroom window, he's yours, and if he don't, he's mine."

"All right," Bobby said, and took in several deep breaths. "I haven't killed anyone since we were in the army. But that was in wartime, and it didn't count."

"What do you mean killing in a war don't count?"

Bobby raised his eyes skyward. "I'm talking about God. Killing is wrong."

"The price on the dude's head is a million bucks, that's worth a little sin."

"Right, okay, I'll head around back." Bobby left the car with his gun tucked against his leg, and ran right, to head around to the rear of the L-shaped building.

After gathering his courage, Derrick left the car and went over to stand outside Tanner's door. When what felt like a minute had passed, Derrick was readying himself to kick in the door, but then he caught sight of Bobby, who was running back toward him.

When Bobby reached him, Derrick pulled him aside and whispered. "Why aren't you watching the window?"

Bobby grinned before he whispered back at Derrick. "I don't need to watch it. There's a window in the bathroom, yeah, but it's up high and a single piece of glass, stained glass too. There's no way he can get out of there quickly, and if he tries, we'll just shoot him."

"All right, good, good. I feel better about both of us going in anyway. Now, I'll kick the door in on three. One... two... three!"

Derrick laid a work boot hard against the doorjamb and the cheap motel room lock broke free, causing the door to fly open and bounce off the wall to the side of it.

They saw no one.

Derrick leaned down with the shotgun at the ready and looked under the bed. While he was doing that, Bobby checked the room's only closet and found it empty of all but a few clothes hangers. When they were certain there were no other places to hide, Derrick pointed at the bathroom door. It was sitting ajar and showed a dark room beyond.

"We know you're in there, dude," Derrick called out, but there was no answer.

The two men crept toward the bathroom with their guns at the ready, both sets of eyes were locked on the slight opening between the bathroom door and the jamb, searching for any movement.

Derrick whispered to Bobby while never taking his eyes from the door. "I'm gonna push the door open. When I do, reach around inside and hit the light switch."

Bobby whispered back at him. "It sounds good but be ready."

Derrick stood to the left side of the door, as Bobby moved over to the right.

After silently counting down from three, Derrick shoved the bathroom door open with the end of his shotgun. At the same time, Bobby reached inside and flicked the light switch. When nothing happened other than the light coming on, Derrick moved into the bathroom while keeping his finger ready on the shotgun's trigger.

The bathroom was empty.

Derrick and Bobby looked at the empty shower stall, then up at the intact stained glass window above the toilet.

There was no other way out of the room, and yet, Tanner wasn't there.

When Tanner cleared his throat, it caused both men to jerk their heads around. Tanner was holding a pair of Tasers. He fired them simultaneously, striking both Derrick and Bobby in the face with the electrified prongs. He then watched them fall to the bathroom's tiled floor and twitch from the shock they each received. Within minutes, he had them gagged and bound and was backing their vehicle up to the motel room door.

After throwing a blanket over Derrick, he carried him outside and dumped the man into the trunk of his own car, he then repeated the procedure with Bobby, got behind the wheel of Derrick's car, and went looking for a secluded spot.

Tanner needed information, and before they died, Derrick and Bobby would tell him what he needed to know.

2

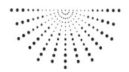

JOB OPENINGS

Inside the remains of a burnt hulk that was once a home, Tanner removed Derrick's gag. Derrick worked his mouth a little, wet his lips, then asked a question that had been driving him crazy.

"Where the hell were you hiding in that room?"

Tanner ignored him while he removed Bobby's gag.

"How did you two find me?"

"We just spotted you," Bobby said. "And it surprised me; they say you're supposed to be in Texas or Mexico."

"Who else knows I'm here?"

"Just us," Bobby said.

"You said that they think I'm in Texas or Mexico, who's *they*?"

"Don't answer him, Bobby. Don't tell him shit," Derrick said.

Tanner reached back, grabbed the shotgun, and pointed it at Derrick. "Interrupt again and I'll kill you."

"It was on the website! Don't shoot! It was on the website," Derrick said.

"What website?"

"At Chemzonic," Bobby said, "It's where we work. It's a chemical plant, and there was an alert for you in the secure area of the website."

"My picture was on an official company website?"

"It's a special website we're not supposed to know about, but the head of security does. I saw him punch in the code once, and so I go on there to take a look every now and then. It didn't do me any good; most of what's on there is encoded. But they had that drawing of you and a one followed by six zeros, so I didn't need to decode what that meant."

"Was it all encoded?"

"Mostly, but under your picture it said something like, se busca vivo o muerto. Consuela in the cafeteria told me that it translated into, 'wanted dead or alive' and that it mentioned a reward, so we figured you were worth a million dollars."

TANNER WENT QUIET AS HE THOUGHT THINGS OVER. The company where Derrick and Bobby worked, Chemzonic, must be linked to the Alvarado Cartel somehow, and in fact, it made perfect sense. The Alvarado Cartel was one of the biggest suppliers of meth. Meth needs precursor chemicals to be manufactured, and what could be better than owning your own chemical plant?

Tanner reached behind him and grabbed an iPad from a duffel bag. After signing on, he asked Derrick how to access the area he was talking about. It was a website that seemed unconnected to the Chemzonic Chemical Company.

"Which link do I hit?"

"Where it says, Members Only," Bobby said.

Tanner hit the link, and a sign in window came up.

"What's the sign in?"

Bobby gave it to him and Tanner saw the drawing with his face on it. The figure $1,000,000.00 was written below it, along with the words, EXTREMELY DANGEROUS! which was written in several languages. The rest of the page was a gobbledygook of scrambled text that made no sense.

"What's the name of the head of security?"

Derrick answered. "He's Jack Rockford, a real pretty boy prick too."

"They wouldn't be hiring on, would they?"

"Maybe," Derrick said. "But Tanner, that's your name right, Tanner?"

"That's my name."

"Seriously man, where were you hiding in that room?"

"I wasn't in the room. I left it right after I entered. I cut out the window in the bathroom when I rented the room and then glued it in place with cheap paste. It pops right out and fits right back in."

"Shit, we should have thought of that."

"Why?"

"Huh?"

"Why would you think of that?"

"You did."

"Yeah, but it's my business to stay alive and that will no longer be a problem you'll face."

Tanner fired the shotgun twice.

There were two new openings at the Chemzonic Chemical plant.

3
INEVITABLE

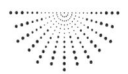

In Mexico, Alonso Alvarado put down his phone after getting updates from the men he had stationed at every border crossing between the United States and Mexico. He would call the men he placed at the airports next, but he didn't expect Tanner to board an airplane, at least not a commercial jet.

He had thrown over a hundred of his best men at Tanner in New York City, and now those men were dead, and Tanner had vowed to travel to Mexico to kill him.

Juan, his only son, had died, and if Tanner made it behind the walls of his compound, Alvarado knew he would join him in death.

Cody Parker, that was Tanner's true name. However, it did Alvarado little good to know it, because Cody Parker had no one left in the world that Alvarado could threaten to use against him. He had already killed the man's loved ones when he thought he had also murdered him.

Tanner was coming to kill him, to avenge the woman he'd lost in New York and for the family he'd watch die years ago. Tanner was coming, and Alvarado didn't doubt it for a second.

He had put the word out about the million-dollar reward for Tanner. The man would be hunted by hundreds of lowlifes, dreamers, and even a few genuinely competent killers.

He hoped one of them might get lucky, or that their combined numbers might overwhelm Tanner, but deep down, Alvarado realized Tanner wouldn't be stopped by such men. No, Tanner was coming, and he was coming for him.

Alvarado had done something a day earlier that he had never done before, nor had ever needed to do. He had hired outside help, professional help, in the form of a company that specialized in security, among other things.

The company was named Hexalcorp. They were supply contractors with several governments, including The United States of America.

Hexalcorp was rated second in their field, but their top competitor, the corporation, Burke, had refused to do business with him.

That slight would not go unanswered, and Alvarado would send grief toward Conrad Burke, the Burke Corporation owner, but for now, Tanner was the main concern.

Hexalcorp was sending a top representative to the compound to enhance the security and had dispatched a group of men they called a "Strike Team" to find and eliminate Tanner.

Alvarado hoped the men would succeed, but he was far more interested in increasing the compound's security, because Tanner was coming. Alvarado knew with everything in him that Tanner was coming, and the bastard Cody Parker was as inevitable as death.

4
CLOSING IN

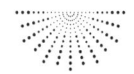

Tanner left the hapless Derrick and Bobby inside the burnt-out house. They would be discovered in the coming days, but not soon enough for it to interfere in his plans.

He dumped Derrick's car in long-term parking at the airport, then took a cab back to the motel, where he apologized for the busted door and paid for its repair. He had enough people after him; he didn't need the cops looking for him over a busted motel room door, and the phony ID he was using was still good.

He drove to a different motel, just in case, and after spending an hour coming up with a revised plan, he sent an email off to Tim Jackson. If anyone could decode what was on Chemzonic's secret website, it would be Tim.

Tanner fell asleep with Derrick's shotgun propped up against the side of the bed. He would sleep until the sun woke him.

The following morning in Mississippi, Alexa was sitting inside her van, watching the sunrise, as she wondered where Tanner was. Her mind told her that he was probably in Mexico by now, but her "little voice," her sixth sense, said that he was heading west, northwest.

She was parked outside a motel and had checked in the day before under the name Anna Sanchez, with a fake ID and credit card courtesy of Damián Sandoval, Alonso Alvarado's rival.

Without doubt, Sandoval was as big a dirtbag as Alvarado was, but his assistance had proven useful, and his man Dante had saved her life.

As she checked in to the motel, Alexa had showed the clerk the drawing of Tanner. The night clerk hadn't recognized him, and Alexa was waiting to ask the day clerk the same question when the new person came on shift.

She took the drawing out and looked at it yet again and wondered what sort of man Tanner was. He was a killer for hire, of that she was certain, but he was also a Tanner.

Alexa's adopted father, her Papa Rodrigo, had known Tanner Five.

Rodrigo had still been a boy of fifteen and living with his widowed mother while Tanner Five had been middle aged, but he had become friends with the man before he knew who and what he was.

Rodrigo was gay, and he and his friends from the circus had been attacked by a gang of local kids from the town where they were performing. After Rodrigo had been spotted holding another boy's hand, the two of them were thrown to the ground and kicked.

Tanner Five had stopped the beating before Rodrigo and his friend were seriously injured, or possibly worse.

Tanner Five had later traveled with the circus and stayed with Rodrigo and his mother for months after that.

Although Rodrigo had never come out and said as much, Alexa always got the impression that Tanner and Rodrigo's mother became more than friends.

In any event, Tanner Five had taught young Rodrigo to fight, at least enough to defend himself, and he had also impressed Rodrigo as being a man of honor.

It wasn't until years later that the two of them met again. By that time, Rodrigo had become an accomplished young thief. Accomplished, but not perfect, and he was caught in the act of emptying a safe by the man he was trying to rob.

Rodrigo told Alexa that after he heard the sound of a shotgun racking a shell, he knew he was dead. But to his surprise and joy, when the blast came, it was the owner of the shotgun who perished, because he had been shot by Tanner Five, who had been hired to kill the man.

The two fled the scene and went where they could talk. That's when Rodrigo learned the truth about his Tanner.

More trouble ensued shortly thereafter, and Rodrigo recounted how Tanner Five went up against incredible odds on several occasions and came out on top every time. He said that Tanner Five told him that he had been trained by his predecessor, the fourth Tanner, who in turn had been trained by his own mentor. A Tanner was an assassin, yes, but they were trained to be more than that, they were trained to be the best, to survive anywhere, and to never give up until the target was dead.

Now, some thirty-odd years later, Alexa searched for her Tanner, and she prayed that he was someone who could help her, and not just some mindless killer.

A car pulled up and parked in front of the motel office. When a man got out holding a paper sack and a thermos, Alexa assumed he was the day clerk starting his shift. She left her van while holding Tanner's picture and went to see if the man knew his face.

~

Alexa lit up when the desk clerk nodded his head affirmatively.

"Yeah, this guy, he was here; it was the night before last. I wasn't working that night, but I was here talking to my boss when he checked in."

"What name did he go by?"

"Oh, I'm sorry, we're not allowed to give out that kind of information, but he checked in alone if that's what you're worried about."

"I'm not involved with him; I'm just looking for him."

The clerk leaned on the counter. He was a young white guy with curly brown hair and gray eyes. He looked Alexa over and smiled.

"He's a lucky guy to have you looking for him, but what are you, some kind of bounty hunter?"

Alexa returned the man's smile and wondered if he was about to hit on her. She would love to know what name Tanner was traveling under, but in truth, it would do her little good. She had no way to track him down electronically and a man like Tanner would change identities the way other men changed clothes.

"I'm not a bounty hunter or a cop, but the man I'm looking for, well, we have something in common. I want to find him to see if we could help each other."

The man straightened up, tapped at the computer keyboard for a moment, and then shook his head.

"He checked out yesterday morning and left no forwarding address, sorry."

"That's okay; thank you for your help."

"You're welcome."

Alexa opened her purse. "I'll be checking out."

"Oh, too bad, I was going to ask you if you'd have dinner with me tonight."

"I might have," Alexa said. "But I should keep moving."

"To find the man you asked about?"

"Yes."

"It's really important to you, isn't it?"

"Yes."

The clerk handed her back her credit card. After a moment's hesitation, he shrugged and gave Alexa more information.

"He checked in under the name of Clay Drake, and I saw him driving a black Ford, a newer model."

Alexa gestured for the man to lean forward, when he did so; she kissed him on the cheek.

"Thank you so much."

"You're welcome, and if you pass through here again, come find me and we'll have that dinner."

"I will."

Alexa left the office and headed for her van. If Tanner had come this far west then he wasn't headed south anymore, which meant she was on the right track. She mentally chastised herself for ever doubting her instincts. When she got back on the highway, she continued to head northwest, toward Oklahoma.

5
RAG DOLL

In Georgia, Ariana O'Grady was in the parking lot of a diner, talking to the waitress who had spotted Tanner days earlier.

The woman had called in her brother and his friends to come and attack Tanner, in hopes of claiming the bounty on his head. Tanner had killed the woman's brother and seriously wounded one of her friends.

Ariana had expected that the woman would want to help her find Tanner, but the waitress, a young redheaded woman named Violet, had only one thing on her mind.

"I'll tell you what you want to know if you pay me ten grand."

Ariana blinked in surprise. She was twenty-seven, with dark hair, a fair figure, and a pretty face, but was usually scowling about one thing or another.

She and her late father, Hank O'Grady, had had their differences of opinion over the years, but she loved her father. When Tanner killed him, she began hunting the hit man to exact revenge.

In truth, Ariana wasn't after Tanner because she was

convinced he had killed her father, but more because it gave her something to do. Before Tanner, there had been her involvement in the war on drugs, prior to that, she championed environmental causes, and while still in college, she attempted to "Save the Whales!"

Ariana hadn't really cared about any of the causes, but they kept her occupied and gave her a reason to get up in the morning. They had also helped her annoy her late father, an activity she enjoyed greatly when she was younger.

Ariana was one of those people who have never wanted for anything materially, and because of it, because of the ease of her life, she felt empty inside and needed something external to fill the void. Tanner was that something at the moment. Chasing after the man was a lot more fun than marching for hours while holding a picket sign.

"Violet, Tanner killed your brother and you want money to help find him?"

"I'm not an idiot, lady. The dude is worth a million dollars. All I want is ten grand for helping you to get him."

Ariana was sitting in the passenger seat of Violet's old car, as Violet was on her break. She turned from Violet and looked up at her companion, a man who went by the name Brick.

Brick actually looked like a brick. He was possibly seven feet tall and nearly as thick as he was wide, even his coloring brought to mind a brick, in that, he was a full-blooded American Indian, a Comanche. He stood by Violet's subcompact car instead of sitting, because his thick frame was too big to fit inside.

Ariana had previously employed four men to help her as she searched for Tanner; the four were mercenaries who came highly recommended. While at a bar in Manhattan, one of the men made a pass at the woman Brick was with at the time, Brick took offense, the other three men joined the fight, and when it was over, only Brick was left standing.

Upon learning this when she went to bail her men out, Ariana left them to rot and bailed out Brick instead.

"Do you believe this stupid bitch, Brick? Tanner kills her brother and all she can think about is money."

Brick gave a nod; he rarely talked.

"Who are you calling a stupid bitch?" Violet said. "And you're damn right I want money. I need it to bury my brother. And you got money, hell yeah you do, shit, that Gucci purse of yours cost thousands by itself."

Ariana leaned closer to Violet. "Tell me what I want to know now, or you will be one sorry piece of white trash."

Violet reached across Ariana and opened the passenger door. "Get out of my car!"

Ariana looked at Violet with a set of cold eyes, but she rose from the car and walked toward her own vehicle, a black Lexus LX.

"We're leaving, Brick."

Brick followed her; his long raven hair was loose and hung halfway down his broad back.

"Don't come back either," Violet said.

~

LATER THAT NIGHT, VIOLET STEPPED OUT THE BACK DOOR while carrying two trash bags, as she headed for the dumpster at the side of the diner. She never made it there. Two large hands took hold of her and lifted her off the ground.

Brick was holding Violet aloft as if she were a child.

One hand was clamped over her mouth and the other was around her neck.

Violet began to panic, but when a sharp pain ran down her spine, she stopped her struggling, fearing that she would hurt herself. She was scared, and wondered if she were about to be raped, but when she saw Ariana come walking toward her from the parking lot with a smug look lighting her face, rage flashed in Violet's eyes.

"Are you ready to talk now?" Ariana asked.

Brick moved his hand away from Violet's mouth and Violet used the opportunity to spit in Ariana's face.

"Fuck you, lady, you and your Indian ape. I ain't never telling you shit for free. And after this, I want fifty-thousand."

Ariana wiped the spittle from her cheek as she stared at Violet in amazement. She thought the girl would be terrified, but no, she was too stupid to be scared. And more than that, she would report the incident to the police.

"Shut her up, Brick."

Brick's hand went over Violet's mouth again.

Ariana stared at Brick with eyes full of indecision. "The dumb bitch will report this as an assault... I don't know what to do."

"Pay," Brick said.

Ariana sneered at Violet. "I wouldn't give this thing a dime if she were starving."

Brick smiled without showing his teeth, then he moved his giant hand up higher on Violet's face until he was covering her nose along with her mouth, and thus, cutting off her air supply.

Ariana opened her mouth in surprise, then watched in fascination as Violet struggled in Brick's grip. The struggle to breathe became frantic, and when Violet tried to swing a leg backwards to kick Brick in the balls, something in her neck snapped audibly, and she went limp.

Brick held Violet off the ground easily while using only one hand, the hand that was around her neck.

Ariana saw Violet's head flop over to the left. When she searched the woman's eyes, she saw only a blank stare looking back at her.

She pointed and laughed. "Holy crap. The dumb bitch broke her own neck."

Brick opened his hand wide and Violet's body fell to the ground, where it lay beside the bags of garbage she had brought outside with her.

Ariana stared down at Violet. Violet's red hair was arranged in twin ponytails and her freckled face had a button nose.

"When I was a kid, I had a rag doll that looked just like her."

"Me too," Brick said.

Ariana looked up at him with her head tilted slightly, not sure if he was joking or not. She then shrugged.

"We'll find Tanner some other way."

Brick grunted in agreement, then they were back in Ariana's SUV and leaving the scene.

6
SURVIVAL

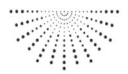

Like Ariana O'Grady, Alonso Alvarado also believed that the violence in Georgia was committed by Tanner. It appeared that Tanner was headed in his direction.

Alvarado was finished with underestimating Tanner. That ended when he realized Tanner was Cody Parker. He had shot an already seriously wounded Cody Parker square in the chest and left him lying on the ground bleeding to death.

On top of all that, the boy was alone and just feet away from his burning house. How Parker survived Alvarado had no idea. He assumed it meant Parker had been helped by someone, in the same way he himself had been saved by his brother-in-law, the recently murdered Carlos Ayala.

As Alvarado thought of the past, he recalled the night he had been attacked, and remembered how his brother-in-law had risked his own life to save him.

MATAMOROS, MEXICO, OCTOBER 1997

. . .

After regaining consciousness, Carlos Ayala rolled over onto his back and felt the edge of his damaged computer dig into his shoulder, but that was not the only source of his pain.

He had bashed his forehead on a stair after having been shot by the intruder dressed in black, and there was a wound on his left side from a bullet. The round had ricocheted off an internal metal component of the computer monitor he had been carrying. Had the shot gone straight through, he would be dead.

Carlos sat up on the landing that led to the second floor. He moaned from both the pain in his side and the sight of his damaged computer. There was also a distressing amount of blood.

The sound of a single shot came from upstairs and Carlos' breath caught in his throat. He wondered if the intruder had just killed his friend and brother-in-law, Alonso Alvarado.

Carlos made it to his feet with a great effort and looked down on the dead guards lying together near the open door that led out to the courtyard.

He could leave through that door and find a safe place to hide until the intruder left, but although he wasn't a brave man, neither was he an abject coward.

Carlos went up the stairs as quickly as he could. His head hurt and his side was burning where the bullet had sliced him open, but fear helped to fight the pain, and he knew he had to aid Alonso if he were able.

The sight of three more dead guards lying outside an open bedroom doorway made Carlos' gasp, but then he heard the voices coming from beyond the closed doors of Alonso's room at the end of the hall. Although both voices were speaking Spanish, Carlos detected an American accent in the intruder's voice.

Carlos was standing in the hall and gazing down at the dead guards when he heard a sound come from the doors leading to Alonso's bedroom. They were being opened; if he didn't hide, the American would know he still lived.

Carlos ducked into the open bedroom doorway just as the left-hand door leading to Alonso's room opened. A few seconds later, he watched as a naked woman ran by, crying, and with her clothes in her arms. It was the whore Alonso had been with, apparently, the American had let her live.

The girl flew down the stairs as the voices resumed inside Alonso's bedroom. There would be more men coming, Carlos had called for them himself, but they would need time to get there. Alonso was trying to buy that time, Carlos realized, as he heard Alonso talking to the assassin casually.

While that was happening, Carlos reached over to the bed and grabbed a pillow. He then slid the pillowcase off and held it to his bleeding side, to put pressure on the wound.

Things must have become violent suddenly, because Carlos heard Alonso screaming in pain as the sounds of a struggle reached him where he hid in the darkness.

Then, the American was speaking again, but Carlos couldn't make out the words. He then smiled as he heard Alonso, and although the voice sounded weak and strained, he was alive to speak.

Seconds later, the American rushed past the doorway and headed down the stairs.

Carlos had just stepped back into the hall to go to Alonso when he heard the American change course and come back up the steps.

He must have realized that Carlos' was missing. Carlos

looked down at one of the guard's fallen weapons and told his hand to reach for it, to pick it up and kill the American. He could not do it. He wasn't a fighter; he was a thinker, an accountant, a man of numbers.

When the footsteps resumed, Carlos realized with a sense of great joy that they were receding and going downstairs, not back up to where he stood terrified, wounded, and unarmed.

He rushed down the hall with the pillowcase clamped to his side and found Alonso lying on his bedroom floor, broken and bleeding.

"Oh my God, Alonso, what did that devil do to you?"

Alonso could barely speak through his broken jaw and his elbows and knees had been shattered by blows. Carlos marveled that the man was still conscious given the pain he must be experiencing, but Alonso Alvarado had always been tougher than most men.

"Help... me... to... stand..." Alonso mumbled.

Carlos got down on the floor. He had just slid an arm beneath Alonso's back when they both heard the footsteps on the stairs. When the footsteps halted, Alonso told Carlos to hide, Carlos did so, by crawling under the bed, an act that made his wound scream. Seconds later, the American ran back into the room.

The man was doing something with a metal can that was making it squeak. Carlos recognized the sound, and his eyes grew large with horror. It was the sound a can of lighter fluid made when you squeezed it. Carlos wondered if the American madman was about to set Alonso on fire.

That was when the man shouted Alonso's nickname while wishing him a hideous fate. The words were spoken with such vehemence and hatred that it made Carlos shiver.

"Burn in hell, Martillo!"

Carlos shut his eyes. He couldn't bear to see his friend burn to death. However, when he heard no screams, he opened his eyes and saw that Alonso looked the same.

An instant later, he realized it was the bed above himself that had been set ablaze, and the room was already filling with smoke.

Fearing he would burn as well, Carlos scrambled out from beneath the bed, as he did so, he saw the American sprint onto the balcony and leap out into the night, to fall into the pool below.

Alonso Alvarado looked afraid for the first time that Carlos could ever recall, and he stared up at him with pleading eyes.

"Don't… leave… me…"

Carlos bit back his fear and reached out to help Alonso. "We are family; of course I won't leave you."

Carlos managed to drag Alonso onto the balcony. By the time he shut the doors on the room, the bedroom was fully ablaze, and smoke rushed from it through a shattered pane of glass in one of the balcony doors.

With strength he hadn't known he possessed, Carlos lifted Alonso up and into his arms. After that, he stepped on a patio chair. The pain in his side increased so dramatically that he nearly passed out, but he kept going and stepped up upon the marble balustrade. After closing his eyes, he leapt as far as he could and landed in the pool.

Both he and Alonso were lying at the bottom of the pool when their men pulled them out of it. After receiving CPR, Alonso was revived. Carlos crawled over to him, and Alonso thanked him silently with his eyes.

The ambulance came just after the fire trucks arrived, and Alonso was loaded aboard. But before climbing on himself, Carlos spoke to Alonso's chief man, who had just returned from a night in town.

"Has the intruder been caught?"

"No, but we will keep looking."

"Call Hector Mercoto and tell him that Alonso has been gravely wounded, as the head of the cartel he will want to know immediately."

"I've already called Hector, and he will be here very soon."

"Good, and you have things under control here?"

Damián Sandoval smiled at Carlos. "Do not worry; I will take care of everything."

Carlos left the estate inside the ambulance, not knowing that he would never step on its grounds again.

In a brazen act that became a legend, Damián Sandoval used the opportunity of the attack on Alonso Alvarado to stage a coup. When Hector Mercoto arrived to see the damage for himself, Sandoval killed the man, and the Mercoto Cartel became the Sandoval Cartel.

Thus, when Alonso Alvarado awakened from his multiple surgeries, he had been not only a gravely injured man and a near cripple, but also a man without power.

7

A GUARANTEE

Alvarado settled into his special chair as Robert Martinez from Hexalcorp was led into his office by one of the guards.

Martinez was fifty-two, an American, an ex-Marine, and a man who would do anything that he thought would further his rise up Hexalcorp's ladder. He oversaw the expansion of the company's business, and in the three years he had held the position, he had nearly doubled Hexalcorp's client base.

He did this by offering Hexalcorp's considerable corporate muscle to anyone who could pay. Most of that new business came from criminals and despots around the world. Hexalcorp's leadership turned a blind eye toward the practice, but Martinez had been warned that all transactions had to be sanitized by being filtered through dummy corporations and third parties.

As long as Hexalcorp appeared spotless, Martinez was given a free hand. It was because of him that Hexalcorp was closing in on replacing the leader in their field.

The leader was Burke, the Burke Corporation, which

held the name of its founder, Conrad Burke, a man who, unbeknownst to Martinez and Alvarado, was an acquaintance of the assassin they now hunted, Tanner.

Malena Alvarado was seated near her husband; she eyed Martinez with an intense gaze. Both she and her husband looked angry and had recently suffered the loss of their son, and also Malena's brother. Martinez knew that if he could deliver Tanner to them, he would have a client for life.

"What is the status of your search for Tanner?" Alvarado asked, as Martinez sat across from him.

"I have a team in Texas just waiting to get a location on Tanner. If the man sticks his head up, they'll chop it off."

"This team of yours," Malena said. "How many men are in it?"

"There are four, and they will find Tanner and kill him."

Malena laughed, and Martinez thought it sounded as if it carried a touch of madness. When the laughter subsided, she spoke.

"Tanner has killed over a hundred of our best men and you send only four after him? That's next to useless."

"With all due respect, Señora Alvarado, I disagree. My team is just that, a team. These men were the best when they served their country overseas and now they are the best the free market has to offer. They've studied Tanner and they understand he's a formidable and very unconventional warrior. They will not be easily fooled or misled as others have been, and they will kill him. It's just that simple."

"I want a guarantee," Alonso Alvarado said.

"A guarantee?"

"Yes, a personal guarantee. And by that, I mean if your

men fail to kill Tanner, you will never leave this compound alive. Do you accept the terms?"

Martinez leaned back in his seat and folded his hands together. This was not the first time he had been asked to pledge his life as a guarantee of his men's success, and it probably wouldn't be the last.

"I agree. But when they kill Tanner, I want all your security business, and I would also like the opportunity to invest with you. I'm sure if I gave you money to invest in your operation that you could triple it in no time."

Alvarado nodded in agreement. "If you kill Tanner for me, you'll never have to worry about money again, and I'll make certain you rise to the top of your company as well."

That last perk was unexpected, and it brought a smile to Martinez' lips. "We have a deal. Tanner will die at the hands of my men. I guarantee it."

Malena stood and stared down at Martinez. "Someone will die, of that we're certain."

~

IN TEXAS, MARTINEZ'S ELITE TEAM OF OPERATIVES WERE cleaning their weapons inside a motel room as they waited to hear word of Tanner's whereabouts.

The four men were Steve Bennett, the Strike Team leader, Roger Wilson, Hakeem Brown, and Mortimer Simms, who just went by Simms because he hated his first name.

They had fought in two wars together and knew each other nearly as well as they knew themselves.

The four men grew up in different sections of America and had vastly different backgrounds, but they were a family as well as fellow warriors.

Bennett, their leader, grew up an army brat and later

joined the Marines. He was thirty-eight, while the others were either a year younger or older than he was. Bennett had dark hair to go along with his good looks, as did Roger Wilson. Wilson had grown up in Los Angeles as the son of a single mother who was a failed actress and an alcoholic.

A black man, Hakeem Brown was rich and the son of a Philadelphia publishing mogul. Hakeem's father had jumped aboard the hip-hop craze early and made millions by creating magazines and websites that catered to the fans of that style of music.

Hakeem was given two million dollars on his twenty-first birthday, but Hakeem was a soldier at heart, and other than the condominium he owned in Key West, Florida, the money went virtually untouched.

Mortimer Simms looked nothing like his name. He was a huge blond guy from Chicago with muscles upon muscles and had competed in bodybuilding contests before joining the Marines after the events of 9/11.

Hakeem reassembled his weapon and checked the slide action. "This Tanner is no joke, Steve. How do you plan to handle him?"

Bennett fed rounds into a magazine as he answered. "I think the way to defeat Tanner is to be patient. The man is a wrecking ball, but even a wrecking ball is harmless once it stops swinging."

"All right, we'll be patient, but what's that mean?" Simms asked.

"It means, gentlemen, that once we find Tanner we do nothing. With the price he has on his head, adversaries will keep coming at him. We will let them wear him down and exhaust his resources before we make our move."

Roger Wilson smiled. "This sounds like what we did in Detroit a few months ago, with the gangbangers."

"That's right, we let them waste their ammo on that

rival gang, lose a few men, and then they were easy pickings. And as good as he is, Tanner is still just one man."

Hakeem slid his weapon back into the shoulder holster he wore. "It sounds good to me. Once we nail him, why don't we hang at my place in Florida. Martinez promised us some time off."

The men all agreed. They were already looking at Tanner as if he were bagged and tagged. They were overconfident; a trait they shared with many of Tanner's deceased enemies.

8

THE FOUR HORSEMEN OF THE RIDICULOUS

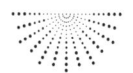

The head of security for Chemzonic was a man named Jack Rockford.

Tanner researched Rockford through an internet search of Oklahoma Real Estate and found Rockford's house. The home was a mansion that resembled a castle and had to be worth millions. Tanner was certain that Chemzonic paid its head of security well, but he doubted they paid that well, at least on the books.

If Rockford was receiving payments for working with or for the Alvarado Cartel inside Chemzonic, it meant he was helping to cover up whatever was going on there.

Tanner guessed that they were manufacturing precursor chemicals that could be used in making methamphetamine, but that sort of thing would be almost impossible to keep hidden from government regulators and plant inspectors.

That would seem to indicate that people were on the take, or maybe Chemzonic had figured out a way to conceal their illegal activities. In either event, Jack

Rockford would have the answers, answers that Tanner could squeeze from the man.

But, why do it?

It would certainly cause Alvarado, who was Martillo, grief, but so would killing the man. And the faster Tanner found Tanner Six and figured out what was going on, the sooner he could continue to Mexico and kill Martillo.

Tanner sighed in frustration. He had tried to reach his mentor but was only able to leave a message for him. That indicated that the man might not be at his home. In any case, he would have to wait for him to make contact. Waiting meant Tanner would be sitting instead of moving. If he was going to be delayed in getting to Martillo, he might as well do something with the time.

Tanner drove past the palatial home of Jack Rockford once more, then headed off to find the man.

~

NEWS OF THE BOUNTY ON TANNER'S HEAD WAS SPREADING throughout the criminal underworld and any punk that learned of it began to fantasize about what they would do with the money.

In Enid, Oklahoma, a biker club calling themselves the Tin Horsemen gathered around a pool table and stared at a drawing of Tanner's face. They weren't really a biker club, but just four guys with motorcycles.

After they realized that the names Iron Horsemen and Steel Horsemen were already in use, they went with the name Tin Horsemen, because after all, they reasoned, metal is metal.

The "club" leader, an idiot going by the name of Scar, jabbed a finger at the drawing of Tanner that was on a flyer, the flyer stated that Tanner was worth a million dollars.

"We're gonna find this dude and get that money."

The other three men all nodded in agreement. They did that a lot. If Scar had pointed at an old wanted poster of Billy the Kid, the men's reaction would have been the same. They were followers and had been following Scar around since the third grade. They would probably continue to follow Scar until the day they died. Given that their current target was Tanner, their deaths could be imminent.

Like Scar, the three men went by nicknames. They were Wound, Bruise, and Abrasion. Abrasion considered himself the cerebral one of the group, but he had a double-digit IQ like the rest of them.

The four idiots were all twenty-one-years-old. They had gone through life trying to get as much money as they could, without having to work for it. They lived together in a converted garage behind a home that belonged to Scar's mother, and they routinely raided the house for food. The poor woman's food bill was more than her mortgage, but she loved her son and had always given him anything he wanted. Since she wasn't rich, that consisted of a drafty garage and free food.

The four wannabe bikers also shoplifted on occasion. Their lives of petty crime had started in high school, where they used to extort money from their fellow students by charging a protection fee. If you failed to pay the fee, you would find your locker broken into and your things missing or trashed.

They tried using this tactic in the real world when they dropped out of high school in their senior year. The local mob explained to them in no uncertain terms that they already controlled the protection rackets.

That lesson came with a broken leg for each of them and ended their dream to forge a criminal empire. Now they were considering going after Tanner, and the thought of claiming the million-dollar bounty on Tanner was overriding any semblance of good sense they had.

Abrasion wiped his nose with his sleeve as he spoke. He was on the short side and skinny, as were Bruise and Wound. Scar was taller, and it was this attribute that caused the others to follow him. He had always been bigger than they were, like an adult, and so they assumed he knew more.

"A million dollars, and it says dead or alive, so we don't even have to kill him."

Bruise pointed at Tanner's eyes. "He looks mean."

"He's a killer," Wound said. "So yeah, he's probably mean. But Scar, how are we gonna find this guy? He could be anywhere."

Scar sent his men a crafty grin. "Ain't we somewhere?"

The others thought that over and nodded.

"Well, Tanner's got to be somewhere too, and if he comes near this somewhere, he's ours. All I'm saying is let's be ready for him."

"Ready how?" asked Abrasion.

"Simple, we keep the bikes filled with gas, load up some supplies in case we have to move, and then we'll go hang out at McGinty's. Them mob guys drink there. If this Tanner comes around, they'll know about it, and then we'll know about it too."

Wound rubbed the back of his neck nervously. "Those guys don't like us, Scar, and I don't want my leg broken again."

Scar smiled as he reached in his pocket. When his hand came out, it was holding a hundred-dollar bill.

"My mom hit the number the other day and gave me

some of the money. If we buy them mob guys drinks, they'll let us stick around."

"What number did your mom play?" Bruise asked.

"Um, I think it was 666," Scar answered.

"That's an unlucky number," Abrasion said.

"Not for my mom," Scar said, as he pointed at the flyer again. "But if you want a lucky number, look here, $1,000,000.00."

The four fools grinned at each other. They had no idea who it was they were hunting.

9

HE HAS HIS PRIDE

The Chemzonic plant was a huge complex aptly located on Chemzonic Drive in Oklahoma City.

Tanner told the guard at the security gate that he was there to apply for a job. After he received a visitor's pass, he drove in and parked near the front office. There was a fenced in parking lot near the entrance to the office. It had a gate that slid aside when the right key card was fed into the box that controlled it. Inside that area were nearly twenty luxury automobiles, which must have belonged to the company's corporate elite.

Tanner wondered if Jack Rockford's car was parked in there, but then he realized that Rockford's ride likely didn't match his house, not if he was being compensated under the table.

Despite his title of Chief of Security, Rockford wasn't a CEO or a Vice-president, and wouldn't be given the same perks as the men or women in those positions.

Tanner confirmed this when he walked along a row of parking spaces that were outside the fenced in area. The spaces had names stenciled at the rear of them. Tanner came to one that indicated it was reserved for a, J. ROCKFORD. The vehicle in the slot was a late-model Chevy. It was a nice car in a good shade of blue, but it didn't match Rockford's stately home.

Tanner left the car and went inside. The office looked like most other reception areas of large companies. There were pictures behind the reception desk that displayed an aerial view of the Chemzonic plant, while on either side of that were photos of Chemzonic's bigwigs, who apparently were all white, fiftyish, and balding, including the woman VP of Plant Operations, who had an odd hairline for a female. Tanner shrugged inwardly. Maybe it was something in the chemicals.

There was beige carpeting on the floor of the reception area, a glass coffee table with magazines, and chartreuse vinyl chairs that looked as if they would squeak when you sat in them.

The office also came with a middle aged blonde. She had a face that said fifty, while her taut and tanned body said thirty. She was standing behind the reception desk as she looked through a tall filing cabinet.

The woman welcomed Tanner with a gleaming smile, and the nameplate on her desk proclaimed that she was Trisha.

"Hello, are you here to fill out an application for work?"

"Yes ma'am," Tanner said, and saw the woman frown slightly. Tanner assumed that Trisha hadn't liked his use of the word, ma'am.

"The only positions available at the moment are in the cafeteria. They need someone to bus tables, or to work as a dishwasher, will either of those do?"

"I'll take anything," Tanner said, while thinking that

they'd soon have two positions open in security once the bodies of Derrick and Bobby were found.

Tanner perused the wall of photos near a side window. They were a collage of pictures taken at what looked like a recent company picnic. Some of them had captions, and in one, a large blond man with perfect teeth was smiling at the camera while holding up a trophy.

It was Jack Rockford, or at least it looked like the pictures of the man Tanner had seen on the internet.

The caption read—JACK WINS THE HORSESHOE TOSS FOR THE THIRD YEAR IN A ROW

Tanner turned from the photos and caught the receptionist looking at his ass.

Trisha blushed slightly. "Um, I know what you mean about taking anything. A lot of people are out of work these days."

Tanner pointed at the photo. "This guy with the horseshoe trophy looks familiar. Is he Jack Rockford?"

"You know Jack?"

"Yes, but it was years ago. I didn't know he worked here."

"Oh, yes, he's been here about four years now. Where do you know him from, was it Mexico?"

"Jack was in Mexico?"

"Yes, we have another plant there in Mexico City, and we'll soon be opening another there as well."

Tanner glanced up at the ceiling as if he were trying to remember something.

"Ah man, try as I might, I can't remember the name of Jack's wife."

"It's Cindy. I see her every year at the picnic. She's a sweetie."

"Yes, she is, but listen, never mind the application. I'd

feel weird working as a dishwasher in a place where Jack is such a big deal. I know it's prideful, but it's how I feel."

Trisha smiled sympathetically. "I understand, honey, and I won't even tell Jack that you were here, but listen, they say the post office is hiring."

"Thanks, I'll check it out."

Tanner left Trisha, drove to the gate, and handed the guard back his visitor's pass. From there, he exited Chemzonic Drive and drove across the way to park in the lot of a 7-Eleven. The parking space gave him a clear view of Chemzonic Drive. When Jack Rockford left for the day in his blue Chevy, Tanner would follow him.

∾

IN DALLAS, ALEXA WAS ALSO SITTING IN THE PARKING LOT of a 7-Eleven. She had driven all morning and made the stop for a quick lunch. When she left the parking lot, she was all set to head back to I-20 West, but instead, by following her instincts, she wound up on I-35 North.

She was headed straight for Oklahoma, City.

10
SPENSER HAWKE

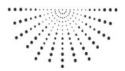

BILLINGS, MONTANA

Spenser Hawke liked to think of himself as a security professional.

The word, "bodyguard" seemed too soft and recalled the image of a man bravely taking a bullet for whoever was paying him to protect them. Spenser wasn't jumping in front of a bullet for a client. He thought it made much more sense to keep the client out of the line of fire. He was doing that now, as he watched the home of Simone Owens.

Simone Owens was thirty-one and the single mom of two young girls. She was being stalked by a dirtbag named Darrell Haney. Haney, a pot dealer, became fixated on Simone when he came upon her in a Casper, Wyoming, supermarket a year ago.

Simone admitted that at first, she was interested in Haney, who was a good-looking guy in his twenties. He drove a nice car and took her out to dinner at a fancy restaurant, but it was over dinner that the crazy came out.

Haney began talking about marriage on that first date and told Simone that they were destined to be together. That was bad enough, but when Haney assured her that she would forget her kids in time, once she gave them up for adoption, of course, she knew that she was talking to a true looney toons.

Simone had been wise enough not to have Haney pick her up from her home, but rather from her place of business. However, when she arrived for work the next day, she found dozens of red roses covering her desk. When Haney showed up a short time later, Simone had to ask building security to escort him outside.

She saw no sign of him when she left for the day, but the next morning he was outside her home and leaning on her car.

Simone had spent months and a fair amount of money going through the courts and dealing with the cops to get Haney to leave her alone. It did no good. She eventually fled from her home in the middle of the night like a thief, with her two children in tow.

That was how she wound up in Billings, Montana, where she found work within a matter of weeks and was starting over. The kids liked their school and she enjoyed her new job and friends.

But ten days ago, Simone came out of her rented house and discovered red roses scattered across the hood of her car. Haney himself appeared shortly thereafter and Simone was about to lose her mind. That was when an old friend named Carrie mentioned Spenser to her.

They had been on the phone at the time, and Simone

thought it strange that her friend insisted on telling her about Spenser in person. Carrie had business near Billings a few days later and met Simone for lunch.

After searching every face in the restaurant to make certain that Haney hadn't followed her, Simone sat across from her friend, while keeping an eye on the entrance.

"So, what's the deal with this Spenser Hawke?"

"He's sort of a bodyguard."

Simone's shoulders drooped. She had tried bodyguards in the past. Haney wasn't intimidated by them. He had even paid some guys to beat up one of the men she had hired.

"A bodyguard won't help, Carrie. Darrell Haney doesn't scare, and I don't have the kind of money where I can pay someone to watch me night and day."

"Spenser isn't your average bodyguard," Carrie said, then she lowered her voice. "He'll make Haney disappear."

Simone's hand flew to her mouth. "You mean he'll... he'll kill him?"

"Yes. When there's nowhere else to turn—call Spenser."

Simone broke eye contact just as the waitress brought their salads and drinks. After the woman left, Simone nodded her head.

"I'll do it. I'll hire him, but Carrie, how much does he charge? After everything Haney has put me through, the lawyers, the move, starting over, I'm practically broke until I sell my old house."

"We used him when George was having that trouble with his business partner, remember?"

Simone searched her memory and came up with a name. "Carl Brown, right? The bastard that embezzled from the business and ran off?"

"That's him, and Simone, he took everything, borrowed more, and left us holding the bag. You want to talk about being in debt; we owed nearly a million. We were about to sell our home and drain the kids' college funds to pay back our creditors. That's when George heard about Spenser from a friend. After we hired him, Spenser tracked down Carl in a week and got back all of our money."

"What did that cost you?"

Carrie grinned. "Not one penny. Spenser took his payment from what Carl had when he tracked him down and gave us back the money we lost. Carl had embezzled from his other partners as well, so I suspect that Spenser made out all right."

Simone looked thoughtful for a moment, then whispered to Carrie. "Darrell Haney is a drug dealer; I bet he has money hidden somewhere."

Carrie nodded in agreement, reached into her purse, and handed Simone a business card.

Simone read the card.

SPENSER HAWKE: WHEN THERE'S NOWHERE ELSE TO TURN—CALL ME!

"Yes, just call the number written on the back and leave a message stating my name. After Spenser calls me and checks that you're legit, he'll contact you."

"What's he look like? He's not scary, is he?"

Carrie laughed. "Oh honey, he's gorgeous, but… there is one thing."

Spenser adjusted his eye patch as he waited for Darrell Haney to show. The forty-something Spenser had lost his left eye years ago but was still deadlier than most men were with two eyes.

Still, he found that he had to compensate for his missing eye and had developed different tricks to do so. One of those tricks was about to come in handy, because unbeknownst to Spenser, Darrell Haney was sneaking up on his blind side.

~

Darrell Haney moved as quietly as he could through the trees at the rear of Simone Owens' home. Darrell had seen Simone enter the house earlier without her kids and assumed she was alone. He was hopeful she had finally come to her senses and gotten rid of the brats, so that the two of them could be together.

But no, Simone was simply playing hard to get again. After scouting out the area, Darrell had spotted the bearded guy with the eye patch. He was smaller than the brutes she had hired in the past, not much bigger than Darrell was really. Once he got by him, Darrell had plans for Simone.

No more foreplay.

Today was the day that Darrell planned to enter the house and take Simone off with him. He had a nice spot all set for her in the basement of a private home two miles away. Between the steel cage and the chain he would place around her ankle, he'd never have to worry about being separated from Simone ever again.

Darrell ducked down as the bearded man glanced his way, and when the guy turned his head again, Darrell crept closer.

Darrell smiled. Simone couldn't have been serious about staying separated, because if she was, she never would have hired a guy with only one eye to guard her. She must have known that all Darrell would have to do is sneak up on the guy's blind side, and then she'd be his.

When Darrell was ten feet away from the man, he stood, and began easing his gun from his waistband. Eye patch was looking the wrong way with his good eye, and soon that one would close forever.

~

Spenser was looking in the opposite direction of Darrell's approach, but he watched the deranged drug dealer creep ever closer. He was looking into one of the small round mirrors he had fastened in strategic spots, along the trunks of different trees.

Darrell's movements were observed in two of the mirrors, and when Spenser saw the dirtbag reach for the gun in his waistband, he spun around and fired.

The weapon was a Taser. Its prongs sank into Darrell's skinny chest and sent a shock through him. The gun slipped from Darrell's hand even as he fell to the ground. Spenser walked toward him while removing zip ties from his pocket. When he had Darrell handled, Spenser took out his phone and dialed.

Amy answered on the first ring. "You got him?"

"We got him. He wouldn't have come close enough if you hadn't fooled him."

"I'll be right there," Amy said.

When she emerged from the home, she was removing the brown wig she wore to make herself look like Simone.

Amy was thirty-eight, had grown-up in Hollywood, and early in her career she had worked as a makeup artist and wardrobe person. The skills ran in the family, as Amy was the fourth generation to work in the film business. Her great-grandmother had slapped pancake makeup on Charlie Chaplin and other silent film stars.

The good-looking Amy had gone on to be a screenwriter, and showed much promise, but that ended when she became the target of a madman.

That was when she was introduced to Spenser. He made the madman vanish from Amy's life while he stayed in it. The two of them became lovers, and on occasion, Amy helped Spenser set his traps, as she did by pretending to be Simone.

With the wig removed, Amy's own raven hair shined in the sun, and she walked over and stared down at Darrell.

"You'll never bother Simone again; do you hear that, you lunatic?"

Darrell opened his mouth to reply, and Spenser stuck a rag in it, before smiling at Amy.

"You were great, honey. When I saw you leave Simone's car and walk inside the house I thought you were her. Had I not known better, I would have been fooled like Darrell was, you really mimicked her mannerisms well."

Amy kissed Spenser on the lips, then stared down at Darrell. "Do you need help with him?"

"No, you just go see Simone and tell her that everything is all right."

"She'll be relieved."

"They always are, and if they could handle people like Darrell on their own I'd be out of work."

"No, you wouldn't; you'd find something to do, and you can always help out at the store."

"Speaking of the store, how soon do you have to get back?"

"There's no rush with Deedee and my brother there, why?"

"I thought we'd take a—"

Darrell kicked out with his feet suddenly. Spenser leapt out of the way easily and shook a finger at him.

"That's a no-no."

Spenser took a small leather case from an inside pocket of his jacket and removed a syringe from it. The syringe held a powerful sedative. Spenser obtained it from a friend, an anesthesiologist who was also a former client. Spenser jabbed the needle into Darrell's neck, and after mumbling for a moment behind the gag, Darrell's eyes closed.

"As I was saying, I thought we could take a little vacation, anywhere you want to go."

Amy smiled brightly. "Aren't you romantic. Why don't we go south?"

Spenser grinned. "I know what that means, New Orleans, and yeah, I could go for some gumbo."

Amy kissed Spenser again, but this time it was longer and more soulful.

"I'll see you back at the hotel, and you be careful with that one there; he's a snake."

"I'll be careful, and thanks again for the help."

"It's my pleasure. I don't know where people like Simone and I would be if you didn't do what you do. Goodbye baby, I'll be waiting for you."

Spenser watched Amy until she drove off in Simone's car. Afterwards, he went in search of Darrell's vehicle.

He found the van parked on the street behind Simone's house and drove it back to park it in the driveway. After dragging Darrell by his collar, he picked him up and dropped him into the back of the van.

Twenty minutes later, he was at the rundown home Darrell had bought. He had followed him there on a previous occasion. This time he went inside, and he found the cell that Darrell had fashioned for Simone in the basement.

It was a welded wire dog kennel. The type normally used outdoors to keep large dogs in. It stood six-feet high, was four-feet wide and eight-feet deep.

Spenser saw where Darrell had done spot welding to reinforce the original wire welds and had bolted the kennel to the basement floor.

If the heavy padlock on the kennel's door failed, Simone would have still had to deal with the ankle iron attached to the chain that had its other end bolted into the brick wall behind the cage.

Darrell had supplied the cage with a thin mattress, a blanket, and a bucket for waste. Had Simone ever been locked inside the cage, Spenser had no doubt that someday she would have died within it. Simone had contacted him none too soon.

He took a few pictures of it to show Amy and Simone, then waited for Darrell to regain consciousness. While he waited, he located the thirty-two thousand and change Darrell had hidden in a chest freezer. It was jammed down inside a box of frozen fried chicken.

The money was more than enough compensation and would easily pay for the trip to New Orleans as well. While Darrell was still out cold, Spenser went through his pockets. That's when he came across the drawing of Tanner on the wanted poster.

Spenser knew Tanner years ago when Tanner was living under the name of Xavier Zane. He recognized him immediately.

"One million dollars, dead or alive."

Spenser placed the poster in his pocket. New Orleans would have to wait.

Since he had found the money without his assistance, Darrell was no longer needed. Spenser took a second syringe from the leather case. Two minutes after he was injected with the fluid from the second syringe, Darrell's heart stopped beating.

An hour later, Darrell's body was settled at the bottom of a pre-dug grave and Spenser was headed back to Amy.

"One million dollars," he whispered.

Yeah, New Orleans would have to wait. Spenser had new plans.

11

HUH, NOW WILL YOU LOOK AT THAT

Tanner followed Jack Rockford to a bar on the other side of the city where Rockford met with a woman Tanner assumed was the man's girlfriend.

That is, unless Rockford's wife, who the helpful Trisha claimed was "a sweetie" was also a nineteen-year-old with huge chest implants.

Tanner sat on a stool at the bar and kept an eye on Rockford and his girl by looking at them in the mirror. He was unaware that he was being watched as well.

It was the bartender, a man named Eddie. Eddie had one of the drawings of Tanner sitting beneath the bar. There was a shotgun there also, but Eddie wasn't a brave man and knew himself well enough to know he could never shoot anyone in cold blood.

However, there was such a thing as a finder's fee, and luckily, Eddie knew just who to call.

In Enid, Oklahoma, Georgie Macateer looked at his phone as he sat in a booth at a different bar, a bar named McGinty's. His cousin Eddie worked as a bartender in Oklahoma City and had surreptitiously taken a picture of a guy he swore was Tanner.

Georgie was a slim guy in his fifties with a full head of curly brown hair. He had never married, loved to gamble, and had essentially taken over his old man's gang when his father went to prison for life back in the 1980's. Georgie's father was dead now, but the gang lived on, and Georgie made a comfortable living while his men did most of the work.

Georgie brought the picture up on his phone. It showed a guy seated on a stool at the bar in Oklahoma City. The man was turned sideways. It could be Tanner or a hundred other guys, but Georgie knew his cousin wasn't a flake. He held up his phone for the other men in the booth to look at the picture.

"My cousin Eddie says that the guy in this picture is Tanner. If that's true, we're looking at a million dollars."

There were four other men in the booth; they were part of Georgie's gang, which had about twenty members. They all made their living with low-level drug dealing and protection rackets.

All four men squinted at the picture, as one of them, a thirtyish thug named Owen, asked a question.

"Why the hell would this Tanner come here?"

Georgie shrugged. "Maybe he's hiding out. I know I never expected to see him in Oklahoma."

"You want to go check it out? It's a three hour round trip."

Georgie thought about that, then stood up from the booth. "We'll go. Hell, it's a million-dollar gamble."

"Should we call in more guys?"

"Nah, either this Tanner is there or he ain't, and if he is, we'll handle him."

Georgie took off with his men and headed south after Tanner.

Following on their motorcycles were the Tin Horsemen, Scar, Wound, Bruise, and Abrasion. They had overheard the conversation between Georgie and his men and asked if they could tag along.

After considering it for a moment, Georgie told them yes. He figured they would make a good distraction for Tanner. That Tanner would kill the four morons Georgie didn't doubt for a second.

That meant that he would not only claim Tanner's bounty, but also rid himself of a minor annoyance. Not bad for one night's work, not bad.

∽

ALEXA WAS IN OKLAHOMA CITY. AFTER VISITING TWELVE other motels, she had located the motel where Tanner had stayed at when Derrick and Bobby tried to attack him. She could feel that she was closing in on finding the man but hoped she wouldn't be too late.

The motel clerk was an old lady and a talker. She told Alexa about the busted door lock on Tanner's room, and said he was a gentleman for bringing it to her attention and paying for it.

"Normally, the guests just check out and don't say anything, then the management wants to blame me. But not your fella, he was a good guy and spoke right up."

Alexa shook her head. "We're not involved. He's... more like a friend."

"A friend, hmm? Well I wish he had gotten friendly with me. It's too bad he didn't have a thing for old ladies or I'd have dragged him into one of the rooms."

Alexa laughed and thanked the woman for her help. She left the office, climbed into her van, and headed for the highway to go north, but at the first traffic light she came to, she felt the urge to drive east instead.

Alexa ignored the feeling, and after leaving the city, she headed north, eager to catch up to Tanner. When she had driven another twenty miles, the urge to turn back grew too strong to ignore. When Alexa finally U-turned, she felt as if she had just scratched a mental itch.

Upon her return to the city, she headed deeper into its center. If Tanner was still in Oklahoma City, Alexa wondered what it was that was keeping him there.

She began visiting more motel parking lots, hoping to spot Tanner. When she reached the parking lot of the seventeenth motel she visited, something inside her told her to pull over.

Alexa looked around the parking lot of the motel and saw numerous cars, a young couple with a baby, and an elderly couple returning from dinner, but no Tanner. Still, her "little voice" was telling her to stay put, so Alexa opened a bottle of water, nibbled on a protein bar, and waited.

Behind her and three doors down was Room 32. It was Tanner's motel room.

∾

TANNER FOLLOWED ROCKFORD FROM THE BAR AND TO HIS girlfriend's apartment. Only an hour after entering the girlfriend's apartment, Rockford came out with a smile on his handsome face.

Tanner had backed his rental up to the rear of Rockford's Chevy. He was standing between the two cars and looking into the trunk of his rental when Rockford returned to his car.

"Huh, now will you look at that. If that ain't the damndest thing. Hey buddy, come take a look at this."

Rockford hesitated for a moment, but he saw the puzzled expression on Tanner's face and grew curious about what could be in the trunk. When he walked over and gazed down into it, he saw nothing. However, after Tanner smashed him on the back of the head with a leather sap, Rockford briefly saw stars.

Rockford's knees buckled, and Tanner guided his torso into the open trunk, then afterwards, he shoved in his legs. After looking around and seeing that none of the three people about had noticed what had just happened, Tanner calmly bound Rockford, covered his mouth with duct tape, and slammed the trunk lid closed.

Rockford had been holding his keys when he was hit. Tanner picked them up from the ground and moved Rockford's vehicle into the parking lot of an adjacent apartment complex, so that Rockford's girlfriend wouldn't wonder why his car was still parked outside. With that done, Tanner returned to his vehicle and drove off.

When he regained consciousness, Rockford would talk, oh yes he would, and with the information he supplied, Tanner would cause Alonso Alvarado, AKA Martillo, more grief.

It would also let Martillo know of his whereabouts, but that was all right, because before the man could act, Tanner would be with his mentor again, with Tanner Six, and the two of them would come up with a plan to bring the bastard down.

Tanner grinned. It would be like the old days all over again.

He drove to the outskirts of the city as he searched for an appropriate place to torture and thought about the coming days.

12
GUTLESS

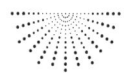

Tim Jackson had left a message for Tanner in his email account. It contained a decoded copy of what had been on the website Chemzonic covertly used.

Nothing much was on the Chemzonic website that was on its surface incriminating, as even the decoded language was riddled with hidden meanings and euphemisms. It was enough to convince Tanner that there was something rotten going on at the plant. Tim had uncovered two other things that were interesting.

One was the wanted poster of Alexa, who was worth a hundred grand dead or alive.

The poster listed her "crimes" and Tanner was impressed. He had been told by Rico Nazario that Alvarado's desert compound was impenetrable, and yet, Alexa had not only made it inside, but had also, as the poster put it, "blasphemed" against Alvarado.

Tanner didn't know what was meant by that, but he assumed he would be pleased by it. He also liked the drawing of Alexa. If she were half as beautiful as the sketch, she would be a looker.

There was yet a third drawing on a wanted poster, one that worried Tanner even more than the one with his own face on it.

It was of Tanner Six, with the age updated, and it was close to how he looked. Alonso Alvarado must have been searching for Tanner Six ever since their encounter, and he was offering a huge reward for information about his whereabouts. Tanner Six was unaware of that, as had been Tanner, because they had both assumed that Martillo, who was Alvarado, was dead.

Alonso Alvarado had to die for what he did to Tanner's family, for Sophia, for placing a price on Tanner's head, and to keep Tanner Six safe. Tanner would kill the man. That was a fact. Now, all he had to do was figure out a way to do it.

He sent another email off to Tanner Six, one which warned him about the price on his head.

∼

WHEN ROCKFORD AWAKENED, TANNER MADE SURE THE first thing he saw was the blowtorch. Rockford screamed at the sight of the flame, and not a manly scream either. There was no one to hear him though, as Tanner had broken into an aircraft hangar on a private airfield. The nearest structures looked to be miles away.

Tanner had secured Rockford to a metal chair after chaining the chair to a support post. The small hangar was spotless, without so much as a grease stain on the floor. Tanner respected the work it must have taken to keep it immaculate.

With that in mind, he had wrapped the support post with clear plastic and covered the floor beneath Rockford's chair as well. When the man bled, it wouldn't leave a trace.

Tanner stood looking down at the big man and spoke to him. "Rockford, I'm not a cop and I don't work for the cartel. My name is Tanner. Maybe you recognize me?"

Jack Rockford tore his eyes away from the flame and stared at Tanner. Seconds later, liquid pattered unto the plastic beneath Rockford as he urinated on himself. When that display of cowardice was done, the man threw up.

Tanner backed away and gazed down at Rockford in disgust. The man was terrified, and Tanner hadn't even begun the questioning yet. Tanner turned off the blowtorch and sat in a chair across from Rockford.

"Tell me what's going on at Chemzonic."

Tears began streaming down Rockford's face. The big blond Adonis looked like a former NFL quarterback, but he was nothing but a wimp.

"You're going to kill me," Rockford moaned.

"If you answer every question truthfully and do what I say I won't harm you."

"Then the cartel will kill me instead."

Tanner shook his head at Rockford in bewilderment. The man had chosen to go into the wrong business. If you were going to work with a drug cartel to manufacture meth, it would be helpful to have an actual set of balls.

"Rockford, once you tell me what's going on, I'll contact the authorities. They'll stick you in witness protection."

"Alvarado owns people here, important people, maybe even Feds."

"I won't contact the Feds here, just in case. You'll be safe, and if you don't cooperate, I'll kill you now. It's your choice."

Rockford sniffled. "Some choice… what is it you want to know?"

Rockford told Tanner everything. He even disclosed the illegal activities that were taking place at the Mexico City plant.

Tanner freed his hands and had him write everything down. It took over an hour. When it was done, Tanner secured Rockford's hands again and gagged him. He wanted to get away from the man.

The dried puke smelled heinous and Tanner suspected that Rockford had not only urinated but had soiled himself as well.

"I'm leaving, but someone will come for you. That someone will be a federal agent. Try to back out, don't cooperate, and we'll see each other again. Do you understand what I mean?"

Rockford nodded.

"Good, and don't worry, Rockford, they'll stick you in witness protection and give you a new life."

He began mumbling, and Tanner loosened the gag.

"What is it?"

"Does my wife have to come with me when they give me a new life?"

"Yeah, or else she'd probably get killed just for the hell of it."

Rockford sagged. "Damn, now I'll be stuck with that bitch forever."

Tanner put the gag back on. It seemed that not everyone thought Cindy was a sweetie.

13
CONTACT!

Cousin Eddie, the bartender, had gotten a look at what Tanner was driving, so Georgie knew the plate number of Tanner's rental.

Tanner had paid cash at the bar for the two beers he'd consumed while there, and so unfortunately, they couldn't get a name off a credit card.

No matter. If Tanner was at a motel, they'd find him by morning. But luck was with Georgie, and a sharp-eyed Owen spotted Tanner as he drove past them while they were stopped for a light.

"Georgie, that was Tanner that just went by, hang a left."

Georgie had to wait until traffic passed by, then he made the turn while the light was still red.

~

Tanner drove into the parking lot of his motel and made a quick circuit around the cars. Alexa remained unseen, because the windows of her van were tinted, but

Tanner took note of the vehicle as he left his car. When the driver side door of the van opened, his hand was moving toward the gun on his belt.

∞

It's him! I've found him. Alexa thought, as Tanner drove past her van and parked.

Tanner was already out of his vehicle and in front of his motel room door when Alexa left her van. She walked toward him at a quick pace. When she saw him reach for his gun, she held her empty hands in front of her.

"I'm unarmed, and, I think we can help each other. My name is Alexa Lucia."

Tanner stared at her with a perplexed expression. It was the woman from the wanted poster, from Mexico, he was sure of it. But if so, what was she doing here?

"How did you find me?" Tanner asked.

Just then, Georgie pulled into the lot. His car was followed by Scar and his gang on their rumbling motorcycles. Georgie stopped the car short and stared at Tanner and Alexa. Although they weren't standing close together, he could tell they had been involved in a conversation.

Georgie thought that Alexa looked familiar and that she might mean something to Tanner. When Scar pulled up alongside of Georgie's car, Georgie pointed at Alexa.

"Get that girl! We can use her."

Tanner opened the door to his motel room as Georgie drove toward him, but before entering, Tanner shouted to Alexa.

"Run!"

Alexa didn't run. She was a fighter. As the Tin Horsemen jumped off their bikes and headed toward her,

Alexa positioned her feet in a defensive stance and took out her knives.

~

Spenser Hawke arrived home in Wyoming after dropping Amy off at her store in town. Amy had not been happy about the cancelled trip to New Orleans, and she didn't understand why Spenser wanted to go after Tanner.

"You're financially comfortable, aren't you? Why risk yourself going after a man like this Tanner?" she had asked.

Spenser couldn't explain it to her, or rather, he wouldn't explain, but the million-dollar reward didn't mean the same thing to Amy that it meant to Spenser.

He checked his messages, and afterwards, he took a shower and sat on his sofa with a bottle of beer to think.

Spenser lived in a home he had built himself; actually, he built it with friends, "his boys" as he liked to think of them. The home had two floors with spacious rooms and an awesome view of the Bighorn Mountains. It was a lot of house for only one man. He had begun to hope that Amy might someday come there to live.

To him, that meant companionship, but to her it meant marriage, and although she spent many nights there, she refused to move in.

Spenser took a swig from the bottle and talked to himself. "Why don't you marry that woman? You know you love her."

Did he love her, really love her? He trusted her with his secrets... well... most of his secrets, but he didn't know how she would handle the big one. The one that made him think about going after Tanner.

He heard the motor while the truck was still a mile

away, because sound traveled well over the empty land surrounding his house. He also recognized the engine and knew it was Amy coming to see him.

He was only wearing a pair of faded jeans and the hair on his chest glistened in the light of the fire he'd built upon entering the house. Spenser padded over to the door in his bare feet and opened it just as Amy stepped out of her pickup truck.

The truck had an emblem on its doors with the name of Amy's store on it, The Trading Post, and she often used the truck to make deliveries. Amy owned the store with her brother, who was also a friend of Spenser's.

In the sky to the north, Spenser saw a flash of lightning and realized a storm was headed his way. He hoped it wasn't a portent of things to come.

As Amy drew closer, he smiled. "Hi honey."

Amy walked over and hugged him. "I didn't like the way we parted, and I didn't want you to think that I was mad at you because you cancelled the trip to New Orleans. I'm more worried about you going after that man, Tanner. He sounds extremely dangerous."

"Oh, he is, that's for certain. But you know that I can handle myself."

Spenser and Amy went inside and settled together on the sofa.

"There's another thing too, Spenser. How do you expect to find him?"

Spenser had been taking a sip of his beer. When Amy asked her question, he grinned around the lip of the bottle.

"Well honey, a man like Tanner will make himself known eventually."

"What does that mean?"

"It means that any dudes that come at him hoping to claim that bounty will not live long enough to regret it. If I had to guess, Tanner will make certain they die memorably. That way, it discourages the next bunch."

"But it won't discourage you, will it?"

"No, but it will let me know where he is, and then I'll travel there and find him."

Amy snuggled against Spenser. "A million dollars isn't worth your life."

"I agree, and don't worry, I'll be fine."

But Amy was worried, and she held Spenser just a little tighter.

14

ALONE AT LAST

Tanner's motel room, Room 32, was bordered by an alley on its left side. He had scouted the area before checking in and realized that the alley would make a good trap, were he to encounter trouble.

Nevertheless, he had planned to use that measure only were he to be pursued by one or two men. When Tanner saw that five men were exiting Georgie's vehicle, he switched to Plan B.

After entering the motel room, he left the door ajar and rushed to a second door on the right side of the room. The door connected his room, Room 32, to Room 33, which was also his room, as he had taken both vacancies when he checked in.

Tanner was through the connecting door in a flash and had it locked before Georgie and his boys hit the door to Room 32.

In Room 33, Tanner cinched a belt around his waist. It was a tactical belt with a pouch on its side. It held several spare magazines, a compass, and a flashlight. But, it was one of the items inside the pouch that Tanner would use.

He grabbed his pre-packed duffel bag from the foot of the bed, even as he removed one of two fragmentation grenades from the belt pouch. Tanner pulled the pin, and after opening the door that led outside, he released the spoon and the grenade armed itself. The countdown had begun.

∽

As Georgie and his men rushed into Tanner's room, Room 32, Alexa found herself surrounded by the Tin Horsemen.

Scar was coming at her from the front, reaching out for her as if she would just stand there and let him grab her. Alexa lashed out with the knife in her right hand and slashed the fool across both palms, then, while still in motion, she kicked to her left and caught Bruise square in the teeth with the heel of her boot.

Scar backed away while looking in shock at his bleeding hands, while Bruise toppled backwards onto the parking lot blacktop.

Being stupid, Wound lowered his head and charged at Alexa like a bull, and like a bull, he wound up gored, as Alexa jammed one of her blades deep into his right shoulder.

∽

Tanner left Room 33 with the lit grenade in his hand. When he looked to his left, he saw Alexa cut one of the bikers while kicking another. The fluidity of her movements told him the woman was a trained fighter. He had to look away from her, because he had his own fighting to do, or rather, he had a toss to make.

The last of Georgie's men had left the door to Room 32 open after entering. Tanner tossed the grenade inside. When it hit the floor, the five men all looked down at it.

∾

Georgie was farther into the room than the others were, as he had been heading to check out the bathroom. When he heard the clunk of the grenade hitting the floor, he turned to look at it, realized what it was, and dived toward the open bathroom doorway.

∾

After lobbing the grenade into the room, Tanner slammed the door shut and crouched down beside the brick wall in the alley.

An instant later, the blast occurred. The windows seemed to billow, and then shattered. To Tanner's surprise, the motel room door had stayed in its frame, although its middle section was missing, along with its doorknob. The side of Georgie's car was filled with pockmarks from the shrapnel and debris.

When Tanner stood, he saw that Alexa had defeated the other two bikers. One had a blade sticking out of his shoulder, while the last one was sitting on the ground and cupping his crotch with both hands.

He smiled. He always liked a woman that could fight.

∾

When the door to the motel room flew open, Tanner drew his gun while wondering how anyone could still be on their feet after such a blast.

It was Georgie. He stumbled from the room like a drunk walking on the deck of a ship in rough seas, then fell face first onto the pavement and breathed his last.

Georgie's backside looked as if it had been fed through a meat grinder, and blood seeped from dozens of small wounds.

Tanner put his gun away, got in his car, and started the engine.

~

Alexa called to Tanner. "Wait!"

But Tanner didn't wait. He had the car in motion even as the door on every occupied room popped open, as the other guests came outside to see what had made the explosion that had awakened them.

Alexa rushed to her van to pursue Tanner, but only after she appeased her curiosity and peered inside Room 32. A second later, she so wished she hadn't looked, as she viewed what a fragmentation grenade could do to several bodies in close quarters.

She was driving out of the parking lot as the desk clerk left the office, and although Tanner had a head start, his car was still in view.

~

As Alexa drove onto the highway in pursuit, she thought about her first sight of Tanner. She had felt something, strong emotions, but she wasn't quite sure what they were.

The sketch had not done him justice, for although the eyes looked like the eyes in the drawing with the fierceness burning in them, there was something else in those eyes as well. It was intelligence, a deep intelligence, and she sensed decency in the man. That he was intelligent had not surprised Alexa, but the sense of decency she felt emanating from him was a shock.

The man was a hired killer, a gun for pay, but then, hadn't she killed as well? Why did she think of herself as a good person? Was it because she only killed those who were in league with Alonso Alvarado?

Yes. It justified her killing, but she was still a killer, a murderer, and she sometimes wondered what her grandmother would think of her. Would her abuela be proud, or perhaps horrified?

Alexa shook her head as she chased away the speculation. Everyone has to live their own life the way they see fit. She didn't regret any of the killing she had done. In fact, she would do much more, hundreds more if necessary. She would kill and kill again until she reached the target of her wrath, Alonso Alvarado. He would die by her hand. She knew this the way she knew her own name.

She was Alexa Cazares, the last of the Cazares family, but she was also Alexa Lucia, daughter of Rodrigo, her Papa.

She would make herself proud, kill as many as she had to kill, and then stand for sentencing come judgement day. And whatever her fate in the afterlife, she would face it with her chin held high.

∼

TANNER LOOKED IN HIS REARVIEW MIRROR AND SAW THAT the van was gaining on him. He nibbled at the inside of his cheek as opposing emotions plagued him. One side of him was telling him to stop the car and talk to the woman, while the other side was concerned about her very presence.

How was it possible that she had found him? Was she even looking for him, or was it all some huge coincidence?

He shook his head. Her appearance at the motel where he was staying would be too big a coincidence, but wasn't she wanted by Alvarado as well?

Again, he was torn by opposite desires. Get away from the woman, lose her, or pull over and talk to her and get answers.

He soon realized that the matter was going to be taken out of his hands, as the car began to slow on its own. When he looked down at the gas gauge, he saw that the tank was empty.

He had nearly half a tank left when he left the motel, but then he realized what must have happened. It was the debris from the grenade blast. A piece of it must have punctured his gas tank.

He brought the already coasting vehicle to a halt, got out, and walked around to the passenger side, where he bent over and saw half of the motel room door handle sticking out of the fuel tank.

The woman, Alexa? Yes, she had said her name was Alexa. The woman's van was drawing nearer. Tanner took out his gun covertly, so that no one in the passing cars would see it, then he watched as Alexa pulled up and parked behind him on the shoulder.

She showed him that her hands were empty, then stepped out of the van slowly. When she walked around to the front of it, they both gazed at each other until Alexa broke the silence. She spoke to Tanner in English, which displayed her Spanish accent.

"My real name is Alexa Cazares, and Alonso Alvarado

killed my family when I was just a girl. I'm going to kill the bastard, and I would like your help, Tanner."

Tanner placed the gun behind his back, in his waistband. After grabbing his things from the car, he walked toward the van.

"Let's go someplace where we can talk."

Alexa pointed at his car. "What about that?"

"It's not working, and it's burned anyway, just like the ID I used to check into that motel."

When they were both sitting in the van side by side, they looked at each other again without speaking; then, Alexa placed the van in gear and headed down the highway.

15

WOUNDS, NEW AND OLD

Scar sighed with relief as he rubbed ointment between his slashed palms before bandaging them.

He and the other Tin Horsemen were in the parking lot of a 24-hour drugstore, tending to the wounds Alexa had given them. Abrasion had gotten off easy with just a kick to the balls, but he was still so sore that he could barely ride his motorcycle.

Bruise had a missing tooth and a split lower lip from the kick he received. He was busy wrapping a bandage around Wound's shoulder. Scar had yanked the knife out of it to the tune of Wound's howls. After slathering an entire tube of antibacterial cream on the deep cut, Bruise was attempting to wrap it tight to stop the bleeding.

Scar shook his head in disgust. A woman, a woman had kicked their asses, and not some Amazonian broad either, but a woman hot enough to be in a centerfold.

"We gotta find that bitch," Scar said.

Bruise nodded in agreement and held up a flyer with a drawing of Alexa on it.

"She's worth money too. This flyer was in Georgie's car. I also got his phone; it was left on the dashboard."

Abrasion spoke as he massaged his balls through the fabric of his jeans. "You stole Georgie's phone?"

Bruise laughed, and the missing tooth in the front of his mouth made him look even dumber than usual. "He don't need it. Hell, you saw him, Tanner blew him to bits."

Scar held up his bandaged hands. Like everything else he'd ever attempted, he'd done a piss poor job of wrapping his cuts. The ends of the bandages hung loose and blew in the breeze.

"New plan; we leave Tanner alone and go after the woman. She might be worth a lot less, but I think we can take her... and I don't want to get blown up."

"That's fine by me," Abrasion said, and the others agreed.

"I'll know that van again if I see it," Bruise said. "It had all them tinted windows and new tires."

Scar straddled his bike. "All right, we'll look for her in the morning. First, let's get a motel room for the night."

"With what?" Wound said. "We spent most of that money your mother gave you on buying gas and supplies."

Scar reached in a pocket with just his fingers, so he wouldn't hurt his hand. When his fingers came back out, they were holding a credit card.

"This is my mom's card; she won't care if I use it."

The four of them rode off to find a place to stay, not knowing that Tanner and Alexa were just a few miles away.

∼

After spotting a nearly hidden driveway on a back road, Tanner had instructed Alexa to pull the van over.

What had caught his eye was the stack of white plastic wrappers.

Each wrapper held a bundle of flyers from local merchants and supermarkets. They were piled in front of an oak tree and behind a hedge that was a few feet past the entrance to the driveway. There must have been dozens of them.

Once parked, Tanner told Alexa he was going to check out the house and to keep the engine running so they would be able to move quickly if they had to.

Alexa said that she would, and Tanner disappeared into the darkness. When he returned just a few minutes later, he told her the house looked lived in, but that there appeared to be no one at home. All the lights were off, despite the vehicle parked under a carport.

"I rang the bell and then went around to the back door and knocked hard on it. If we're lucky, whoever lives here is away on vacation."

Minutes later, they were inside the home. Alexa had picked the lock on the rear door in the kitchen like it wasn't even there. Once again, Tanner had been impressed by her.

The home sat back from the road and was surrounded by trees on three sides. The fourth side opened onto a large field that stretched for over a mile. Beyond that was a roadway, discernible because of the lights of the vehicles moving on it.

Upon entering, both Tanner and Alexa wrinkled their nose. The house had a musty odor. To the relief of both of them, the electricity was still on, and they looked around the kitchen.

A newspaper sat open on the table as if someone had just been reading it, and there was a coffee cup sitting beside it. Tanner looked inside the cup and saw a dark sediment at its bottom, as Alexa pointed at the newspaper.

"Look at the date. This paper is over four years old."

Tanner took out his gun and motioned for Alexa to follow him. There was no door between the kitchen and the hallway, but beyond the threshold, the home looked dark.

Alexa handed Tanner a small flashlight from her purse, and he shined it into the hall. He held it in his left hand with his arm extended out from his body. If someone were to fire at the light, he might have a wounded hand, but the rest of him would likely be spared.

However, nothing happened, but there was an open door across from the kitchen entrance. When Tanner moved closer and shined the light that way, a set of wooden stairs were revealed.

With his gun at the ready, Tanner stepped to the opening and shined the light down the steps. That was when he and Alexa saw the body lying at the foot of the stairs.

They moved away from the basement, and Tanner shined the light about the hall.

Alexa spotted an odd sight by the front door and silently pointed it out to Tanner. After looking at it for several seconds, Tanner moved back to the basement and tried turning the light on. Nothing happened, and he thought that the bulb must have burned out a long time ago. He then played the flashlight beam over the body.

The corpse was desiccated, shriveled, and had been an old man when alive, judging by the white hair visible at the back of its head. It wore khakis and a red flannel shirt, but only one brown slipper.

When Tanner moved the beam around, he saw the other slipper. It was lying on the third stair from the top and blended in with the dark wood. He then shined the beam back at the pile of envelopes lying against the front door and knew what had happened.

Alexa had figured it out as well, and she spoke it aloud. "The old man fell down the stairs… a long time ago. How is that possible?"

"It happens now and then. I once read of a man who died of a heart attack in his apartment and wasn't discovered for over six years. All his bills were on auto pay, even his rent. He was found sitting in front of his television when a pipe burst in the apartment and had to be fixed."

"Still, didn't someone miss him?"

"Apparently not."

"How sad."

"Let's check the rest of the house, just to be sure."

It took only a few minutes to confirm that they were alone. There were no pictures in the house, or at least none visible. Alexa wondered what sort of lonely existence the old man had lived.

Once they were back in the kitchen, Alexa opened the refrigerator, then closed it quickly. The smell inside was horrible.

"Everything in there needs to be thrown out," she said.

Tanner took a seat at the table and gestured at the chair across from him.

"Tell me your story. What did you mean when you said that Alvarado killed your family?"

Alexa sat, folded her hands in front of her, and began her tale.

"I was seven, and it was my tía's… my aunt's birthday."

Tanner held up a hand. "If it's easier for you, you can talk to me in Spanish. I speak it fluently."

"Do you? That's good, and yes, I think more clearly in Spanish."

Alexa began talking again, in Spanish. When she reached the part where the trucks full of men arrived, Tanner felt a chill run down his spine.

16

KINDRED SOULS

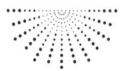

Jack Rockford had been strapped into a chair for so long his legs had gone numb.

He had drifted off to sleep once and wondered if he had done so a second time, as the sound of an approaching vehicle stirred him and made him jerk his head up.

He prayed it was the cops and not Tanner returning. Tanner was as bad as the cartel street hoods, and must be worse, since he had supposedly killed so many of them.

The vehicle, which sounded like a car, drew closer, stopped moving, and then Rockford heard the engine cut off. Whoever was out there was being cautious, because they didn't just walk into the hangar, but must have been looking things over.

Finally, the small door built inside the massive hangar door opened, and a man entered carrying a gun. The man was very handsome, and there were FBI credentials dangling from a chain around his neck. He also looked tired. Rockford briefly wondered how far the man had traveled to get to him.

When the gag was removed, Rockford wet his dry lips

with his tongue and looked up at the man. "I'll tell you anything that you want to know, but you have to protect me."

"Protect you from the Alvarado Cartel?"

"Yeah, and Tanner too."

Special Agent Jake Garner of the FBI field office in New York City listened as Rockford talked. Tanner had faxed him Rockford's confession, and he immediately made the trip to Oklahoma on the strength of it.

As he listened to Rockford in person, Garner realized he would likely get a promotion from the bombshell info Rockford had. And in his mind, Garner sent Tanner a silent thank you.

∽

ALEXA FINISHED HER STORY. SHE HAD EVEN MENTIONED Rodrigo by name and told Tanner that he had known Tanner Five.

Tanner had listened without making a comment, but he realized that if her story were true, they were kindred souls and fellow sufferers at the hands of Alvarado.

After taking a deep breath, Alexa switched back to English and asked a question.

"You are the sixth Tanner, correct?"

"I'm the seventh. Your Tanner trained my mentor."

"Why are you in Oklahoma?"

"Why do I have to have a reason? Maybe I just came here to hide."

Alexa laughed. "A Tanner doesn't hide from anything. That's what my Papa says, and you have done nothing but proven him right."

"I have to get to my mentor, Tanner Six. He's had dealings with Alvarado years ago… and we both thought the man was dead. We only knew him by his nickname, Martillo."

"Hammer... he used a hammer to murder my grandmother."

"How did you track me down?" Tanner asked.

"The short answer is... I'm psychic."

"Psychic?"

"You don't believe in a sixth sense?"

"Maybe I do, but I call it following my gut."

Tanner was leaning back in his seat, and Alexa's eyes flowed over his torso as she smiled.

"I don't see a gut; you look very fit to me."

Tanner stood. "There are bedrooms upstairs."

Alexa raised an eyebrow. "Yes, and?"

Tanner smiled slightly. "And I thought you might like some sleep, alone. I wasn't suggesting anything. I'll sleep down here on the sofa."

"I know, I didn't mean to... never mind, but maybe we should take shifts, no?"

Tanner pointed toward the front of the house.

"That's a gravel driveway out there. If a vehicle drives on that I'll wake up, but I'll also set up temporary alarms on all the doors and windows down here. Still, it's very unlikely that we were followed."

"I see your point, but I have to go out to my van and get some things before I settle down for the night."

"Fine," Tanner said, and then the two of them just stared at each other. They had done so several times already. And while those glances and stares were fueled by suspicion or wariness, this one was fueled by admiration. They were attracted to each other. Each one felt it and knew the other was feeling it as well.

Alexa gave herself a little shake and broke the spell. "I'll be right back."

They cleared the mail away from the front door and saw that it looked to be mostly junk mail, and that there were no personal letters in the pile. There was an old desktop computer on a table beside a console TV. Tanner guessed that the old man had paid everything on line and likely had his bills deducted automatically.

If there was still a large sum of money in the man's account, who knew when the body would have been discovered.

Tanner followed Alexa out onto the porch and looked around at the night while Alexa retrieved her bag. He used the flashlight to look at the vehicle beneath the carport on the left side of the home. Its tires were flat after having sat for so long.

There was a shape out in the field. It looked like it might be a shed of some kind, a big one, since it was about the size of a small garage. Whatever it was, it was leaning to the right and in need of repair.

When Alexa walked back to him, she handed Tanner a bottle of water and a protein bar.

"It's not much, but it will do until morning."

"Thank you," Tanner said, and again, they found it difficult to break their gaze.

Alexa walked through the doorway, then looked back at Tanner. "Call me if you need anything. I mean, if you need help with anything, to do with security."

"I'll be fine," Tanner said.

"What should we do with the old man's body?"

"Why should we do anything?"

"I want to bury him."

Tanner thought about it and then sent her a nod. "We could do that. It looks like no one gave a damn about him in life; at least he can get some attention in death."

"Thank you. And we can help each other, Tanner. Together we'll see that bastard Alvarado dead."

"Let me think about it, and as I said, first I have to speak with my mentor."

"Is he nearby?"

"Yes, I should reach him soon."

"Good, I'll come with you."

"Well see, Alexa. Okay?"

"Yes, first we must have trust, I see that, and goodnight."

Tanner watched her walk up the stairs as he shut the door.

Unless her words were all lies, he had found an unexpected ally in Alexa. That was good. And if she were lying, if she were playing him somehow, that would be bad, because it meant he'd have to kill her. Tanner could think of things he'd like to do to Alexa but killing her wasn't one of them.

"I hope you're the real deal," he whispered, and then he went off to secure the doors and windows.

17

TRUTH AND CONSEQUENCES

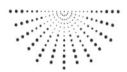

Spenser Hawke had always been an early riser, and the morning after Tanner met Alexa was no exception.

What was an exception was the fact that the power had gone out during the night. He remembered waking momentarily when the thunder began and assumed that the storm must have brought high winds with it.

Spenser threw on jeans, a sweatshirt, and an old pair of sneakers, and went outside to the generator shed. Once the generator was operational, he returned to the house and responded to the few emails he had, then checked for phone messages. He had none, and so that meant that he had no client for the time being. That would change, because someone's back was always up against the wall, and when they couldn't handle their problems themselves, they called Spenser.

He turned on the small TV in the kitchen and watched the news channel while he made coffee.

Amy didn't rise as early as he did, but she still rose earlier than most, and so Spenser knew that she'd be down soon. He wasn't a great cook, but he did know how to make buttermilk biscuits and cook bacon.

He had just placed the biscuits in the oven when the story came on about the grenade blast in an Oklahoma City motel room. According to the report, five men had died, and they had been identified as being involved in organized crime. The police there were speculating that a rival gang was to blame, possibly even a biker gang, since several men on motorcycles were spotted leaving the scene after the explosion.

Spenser turned off the TV. It wasn't a mob hit, or bikers, it was Tanner. He was in Oklahoma, and soon, Spenser would be there too.

~

Amy came downstairs a short time later dressed in a nightgown. After she and Spenser kissed good morning, Spenser pointed at her.

"You already keep clothes here, why not move them all in?"

Amy lowered her head and stared up at him. "Is that your way of proposing marriage?"

"No, but it makes sense, doesn't it?"

Amy said nothing more as she walked over to the counter and poured a cup of coffee. After looking through the cabinet and finding the honey, she sat at the counter and spread some on a biscuit.

"Is it because you don't trust me, or because you don't trust anyone?" she said.

"I don't get your meaning?"

"Trust, Spenser, you have trouble trusting people, or maybe it's just me."

"What do you mean? You know what I do for a living; doesn't that show you that I trust you?"

"Many people know what you do for a living. Every one of your former clients knows what you do... that doesn't make me special."

Spenser left his seat and walked around the table to stand beside her. "Hey?"

Amy looked up at him and he leaned over and kissed her.

"You are special to me; I thought you knew that?"

"All right, then tell me why you want to go after such a dangerous man like this Tanner? Is it a macho thing? Do you want to prove that you're tougher than this Tanner guy? It's not the money, I know that much; you're not the materialistic type."

"One million is a lot of money, can't that be the only reason I want to find him?"

"No, not in this case, because I can tell that there's something personal about this for you. My Spanish isn't as good as yours is, but I saw the word, asesino, on that flyer. That means assassin. Did this Tanner kill someone you loved?"

"No, it's nothing like that, but I knew Tanner when he was younger and went by a different name, Xavier Zane. That's an advantage I have over everyone else looking for him. I even think I know where he might hide out."

"How did you know him? You never talk about your past."

"It doesn't matter; all that matters is now."

Amy tossed the half-eaten biscuit on her plate and stood. "Keep your damn secrets to yourself then!"

She marched up the stairs and returned with everything on but her shoes. When she sat on an arm of the sofa to put them on, Spenser called to her.

"Why are you rushing off?"

"Because I don't stay where I'm not wanted."

"Who said you weren't wanted?"

"Trust! You don't trust me."

"Amy don't go. Just stay and we'll talk."

"All right, talk. Why do you want to risk your life needlessly? You do that enough, you know? But at least when you're working you're helping people who have nowhere else to turn, but this, this manhunt, it's…it's beneath you."

Amy finished with her shoes, grabbed her purse from the entry table, and opened the door.

Spenser came up behind her and slammed it shut.

When Amy turned and glared up at him, he stroked her hair.

"I'll tell you everything."

"Promise?"

"Yes, and then you'll probably never want to see me again."

Amy hugged him. "I can handle truth, Spenser. It's lies I can't stand."

Spenser led her back over to the sofa and began talking. He spoke for over an hour as Amy mostly listened. When he finished, she said she needed some time to think about everything he'd said.

~

As Amy was about to drive off, she asked a question. "When are you going off to find Tanner?"

"I'll leave around noon."

"Why so soon?"

"It's a long drive," Spenser said, and stared at her, and

something suddenly seemed so clear to him. "I love you, Amy. I really do."

"I love you too, but I need time to think. Do you understand that?"

"Yes."

Amy drove off, and Spenser wondered if he'd ever see her again.

18

FRIEND OR FOE?

THE STRIKE TEAM FROM HEXALCORP WAS IN THE AIR AND headed for Oklahoma City. Simms was a chopper pilot. He was speeding them along as fast as he could.

They wanted Tanner as bad as anyone, but unlike the men who were hunting Tanner for money, they were hunting him as a matter of pride. Tanner was a mission to these men, and they had never failed to accomplish a mission.

Their team leader, Bennett, had a plan to engage Tanner only when he was worn down by other, and lesser, opponents. Then, and only then would they strike.

To ensure that Tanner faced many, they had put the word out that he was in Oklahoma City. They had also asked Martinez to have Alvarado raise the bounty. Alvarado did so gladly, and Tanner was now worth two million dollars. As the strike team moved toward Oklahoma, so did scores of other men.

Tanner could run, he could hide, but he could not stay hidden, and once he was worn out from the chase and the fighting, the Hexalcorp strike team would make their move. It was a good plan, and someone else had the same idea.

~

Ariana O'Grady watched the news reports coming out of Oklahoma City on her iPad. Tanner had killed five mobsters who had been looking to cash in on the bounty, a bounty that had recently been raised to two million.

Ariana smiled. It looked like Tanner would be a dead man one way or another with so many people out to kill him, and that pleased Ariana just fine.

She was in the passenger seat, as Brick drove, and to say that the man wasn't much of a conversationalist was an understatement. He barely spoke even when asked a question.

"Tanner is worth two million dollars now, Brick, but don't worry, I'll double your pay. As much as I'd like to be the one to kill him, I'd be just as happy if someone else did the deed, as long as he's dead in the end."

"What else?"

"Excuse me?"

"You said 'dead in the end,' we're all dead in the end. What else is there?"

Ariana turned in her seat and smiled at Brick. "Well, well, you're a philosopher, and that's also more words than you've spoken since I've known you."

Brick shrugged, and then he turned his head and smiled at Ariana. "I like you."

"I ah, I like you too, Brick," Ariana said, as she wondered what Brick meant by "like." Was it like as in friendship, admiration, or could he have meant...? She straightened up in her seat until she was facing front again. The man was three times her size and hardly what one would call attractive. After they had driven a mile in silence, Ariana decided to try to clarify things.

"That woman back in New York City, the one you got in the fight over, was she your girlfriend?"

"No, she was my employer. I liked her too."

"I see, and you two became close?"

"Yes, I left her no choice."

"What?"

"If she didn't sleep with me, I promised her that I would kill her, understand?"

Ariana did understand, and she suddenly wished that her luggage wasn't in the rear of the vehicle, because her gun was in her suitcase.

Without warning, Brick elbowed her in the ribs and laughed. "It's a joke, Ariana; you're not my type, too skinny."

Ariana was relieved, but also angry. "You have a weird sense of humor, Brick."

"Yeah, but I like it."

∼

Before going to sleep the previous night, Tanner had checked his email on his laptop. He was relieved to see a message from Tanner Six. After several emails sent back and forth, they finally decided to meet in person at a rendezvous point.

Tanner Six was stunned to learn that Martillo was alive, and he had no idea how Martillo could have possibly survived.

Tanner also informed his mentor that he too was a wanted man and that there was a sketch of his face being passed around.

Tanner also mentioned Alexa, but he told Tanner Six he didn't know what to make of her yet.

Over the last few days, Tanner had spent hours coming up with various plans to avoid the people hunting him for the bounty, including his usual plan to just kill anyone that tried to kill him.

Tanner Six told Tanner that Alvarado would be sending men to kill him as well, and they would likely be more highly trained than the street soldiers he'd been using.

"The man is many things, but foolish isn't one of them." Tanner Six had written in an email. "He'll likely hire outside help, trained mercenaries, or possibly another hit man. You won't be able to outgun them, but you can outthink them."

Tanner hadn't considered that Alvarado would hire professional help, because the man had hundreds, if not thousands of men working for him. But it made sense, and yeah, if they were good, they would be trouble.

"You've grown wiser over the years." Tanner typed back in an email, as he teased his mentor.

"I still know a trick or two that you don't." Tanner Six had responded. "And Cody, be careful, you'll be going up against a bunch of yahoos, yes, but Alvarado will be upping his game, count on it."

After writing back and forth, Tanner Six suggested a plan. Tanner liked it and wrote back.

"I'm going with your plan. I've grown a little wiser too."

~

WHEN ALEXA CAME DOWNSTAIRS THE FOLLOWING MORNING, she had placed her laptop on the kitchen table and showed

Tanner the news story about the motel, where he had killed Georgie and his men.

"It's being blamed on those bikers right now, but I did see where they interviewed a bounty hunter who said he was looking for you."

"Fortunately, half the people out there think I'm a myth, even segments of the law enforcement community don't take me seriously."

"I grew up hearing the myth," Alexa said. "But my Tanner was Tanner Five."

Tanner headed over to the back door in the kitchen. "Come with me; I want to see what the outside looks like in daylight."

Alexa followed, and they were both surprised to see that the home's lawn looked well groomed.

"I guess the lawn service gets paid automatically as well," Tanner said.

They walked out to the shed and found an ancient motorcycle with flat tires. The bike looked like something from the sixties, and some small creature had once nested inside its leather seat. Besides the ancient green and yellow striped bike and a few yard tools, there wasn't much to see. The shed itself looked like a stiff breeze could knock it over.

Out past the shed, the land soon ended and there was a road with traffic going in both directions. Beyond that was a chain-link fence, and then the rear of a bowling alley.

They walked out front by using the driveway and traveled both ways along the quiet street. There wasn't much to look at but trees. When they walked back the way they had driven in the night before they noticed a stream on the other side, which sat at the bottom of a short hill.

The nearest home was around a curve and on the opposite side. To reach it required driving over a small wooden bridge that had been built above the stream, and beyond that, the home sat back from the road.

In the opposite direction, the road dead-ended where the stream curved westward, and beyond a rusty wire fence was the roadway seen from the field. Tanner walked over to the thick overgrown hedges on the right side of the road, and when he stood on his toes, he could see the dilapidated shed sitting a dozen yards to the right.

When they returned to the house, Alexa gestured out at the wide field. "This must have been a farm at one time."

"Yes," Tanner said, "and now it'll be the place I make my stand."

"You want to stay here, why?"

"If I move I'll be pursued and have no option but to fight wherever I'm attacked, but here, I can control things, and the only way to survive superior numbers is to be prepared."

They walked out into the field again, and once more, Tanner asked Alexa how she had found him.

"I explained that. I simply followed my, well, you would call them hunches."

"That's beyond a hunch, and it makes me think you're hiding something."

Alexa stopped walking and held out her right hand. "Take my hand."

"Why?"

"Just do it. It doesn't always work, but sometimes when I touch someone, I get... impressions. If it works with you, I'll be able to tell you something that I have no way of knowing."

Tanner shrugged and took her hand. He didn't know if she was feeling anything, but he was, and he had to resist the urge to pull her closer.

MORE DANGEROUS THAN MAN

Alexa had shut her eyes, and after nearly a minute passed, she said something that shocked Tanner.

"Cody? Does that mean anything to you? I also see the word... Buffalo? Or maybe it's the animal that you're thinking—"

Tanner had jerked his hand free and was grabbing his gun from under his jacket, but as he was bringing it up, Alexa kicked at his hand and sent the gun flying into the air. She then dived for the weapon and caught it before it hit the ground.

The act had placed her on her knees, and she sensed Tanner coming up behind her. She kicked out once again, and just barely managed to catch Tanner with a sweep kick that took his legs out from under him. She then stood and pointed the gun at Tanner where he lay on the ground.

She had his gun and had thought him defenseless, but he was a Tanner she reminded herself, and she gazed with trepidation at the grenade clutched in his hand.

The grenade was in Tanner's right hand, while its pin was held in his left. If Alexa shot him, he would release the spoon, the safety lever, drop the grenade, and take her with him.

"What the hell is wrong with you, Tanner? Why did you try to shoot me?"

"What you said, there's no way you could know that, that is, unless you were working for Alvarado."

Alexa turned red with rage at the accusation. "I would die before helping that man, and what was so special about what I said?"

Tanner gazed up at her. "You said, 'Cody' and then the word 'Buffalo' what were you talking about?"

"I don't know why I said those words, but they were there in your mind."

Tanner hissed through his teeth. He wanted to trust

this woman, and he did believe in a sixth sense. He himself had displayed such a nature at times, even though he thought of it as following his gut. There was also Nadya, Romeo's wife, who had exhibited a talent for seeing the future on more than one occasion.

"If you're the real deal, lady, you have a scary gift."

Alexa sat the gun on the ground beside Tanner.

"You can trust me, and there's no one on earth who wants to kill Alonso Alvarado more than I do."

Tanner carefully placed the pin back in the grenade. He then picked up the gun, slid it into its holster, and stood. He walked over to Alexa and saw that she appeared nervous, but unafraid.

"Tell me something else," Tanner said.

Alexa raised her chin up. "If I can, I will. What would you like to know?"

Tanner smiled. "Where would you like to go for breakfast?"

19

ESSENTIAL ITEMS

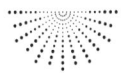

Alexa and Tanner had agreed it was best to grab breakfast from a drive-thru window, and after they ate, Tanner went shopping inside a superstore that carried nearly everything.

Alexa followed along and was both fascinated and puzzled by many of the items he bought, such as the matching set of work clothes that came in a hideous green color, and the clipboard and cheap calculator.

While they walked through the aisles, Alexa went about the market loading a cart with food and other household supplies. She was a decent cook and was tired of eating fast food.

In the cleaning aisle, Tanner gathered soap, bottles of ammonia, and other chemical cleaners.

She assumed he would use the items to make a bomb of some sort if needed, and when they entered the home improvement department and bought galvanized pipe, a hacksaw, and boxes of nails, she was sure her hunch had been correct. She hadn't asked any questions.

Tanner wore a baseball cap with a long bill to block his

face from the cameras most stores had, while Alexa had donned a hood.

When they entered the electronics department, it intrigued Alexa. When Tanner loaded security cameras into the cart, she assumed they would be setting up video surveillance, although she had expected him to be gathering items that were more of an offensive than defensive nature. Still, she said nothing.

However, when he grabbed three packs of condoms off a rack, Alexa felt the need to ask a question.

"Do you have plans that I should know about?"

"There's no plan, but I live in hope."

Alexa laughed as she shook her head in wonder. "Do you have any idea how many people want to kill you, and this is what you're thinking of?"

"I can put them back," Tanner said.

After staring at each other for a moment, Alexa grabbed the condoms from his hand and tossed them in the cart.

"What else do we need?" she asked while walking away, and behind her, Tanner grinned.

"I think we're good, but when we get back we've a lot of work ahead of us, and I doubt we'll finish early."

"Once we get back to the house, I want you to explain everything to me."

"I will, but I'm hoping to not need most of this. Still, it's better to have it than not have it."

"I still want to know."

Tanner nodded at Alexa. He wasn't used to having a partner, but she deserved to know their plans. He had also liked that she hadn't pestered him about every item he bought.

"I'll explain everything when we get back, but you

should know, Alexa, you might be safer staying on your own."

"Alvarado wants us both dead, and it's mutual. We stay together and kill the bastard, or we die together."

Tanner looked her over. She was all woman, but she had the heart of a fighter.

"Why are you staring at me?"

"Two reasons?"

"And they are?"

"One, I'm impressed by your courage."

"And the other reason?"

Tanner smiled and then his gaze fell upon the boxes of condoms.

Alexa laughed and laid a hand on his chest. "If we survive this, we'll explore that second reason."

Tanner took the hand that was placed on his chest and gave it a gentle squeeze. "We'll survive."

Alexa had smiled in agreement. Tanner released her hand, and they left the store and went off to prepare for war.

∼

SPENSER WAS GETTING SET TO GO TO OKLAHOMA WHEN Amy came driving in from the road. After their earlier conversation, Spenser wondered if he would ever see Amy again.

When she left her vehicle, Amy was carrying a suitcase. Spenser first feared she had brought an empty bag along to have something to pack her things in, but no, he could tell by the way she was handling the suitcase that it already had weight inside it.

"I'm coming with you, Spenser."

Spenser met her several feet from his truck and took the bag from her.

"That means you're sticking with me?"

Amy smiled, and then she kissed him. "I love you, and I'll take you as you are, all of you, your past included."

They hugged, then Spenser gestured at her bag. "I'm glad you're with me, but I don't think you should go on this trip. It will be dangerous."

"Yes, it will, for you, and I'm not going to let you face that alone."

"All right. I know better than to try to talk you out of something."

As they were about to leave, Amy asked how long a drive it was to Oklahoma City.

"About seventeen hours. I want to do most of it today, but we're not going that far south."

"Where are we going?"

"We're going where Tanner believes he'll be safe."

"And you're sure he'll be there?"

"Time will tell," Spenser said, and then he drove toward Tanner.

20

RESPECT FOR THE DEAD

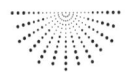

Tanner had agreed to bury the body found in the basement. After digging a hole, he went down there with a sheet to wrap up the corpse. The man had been very old, Tanner could tell, and there were no rings or other jewelry on the body.

When Alexa came down to help, Tanner was surprised, as most people were squeamish around the dead. However, Alexa put on a pair of gloves and helped Tanner to wrap the dead man in the sheet.

"I found some things last night that belonged to him," Alexa said. "His name was Ralph Harper, he was eighty-seven when he died, and he won several motorcycle races back in the sixties. There is a box of trophies in the back of the bedroom closet."

"I guess that old motorcycle in the shed meant something to him," Tanner said.

Alexa nodded. "Yes, I found a box of pictures as well. In several of them he appeared to be riding that green and yellow motorcycle. He had also been married, but his wife and his teenage daughter died in a fire in Chicago in 1974."

Tanner stared at Alexa. "How do you know all that? Did you feel it, sense it somehow?"

Alexa laughed. "No, of course not."

"It wouldn't be any stranger than you finding me the way you did."

"I've always been psychic, but trust me, finding you that way was the most amazing thing I've ever experienced. What I call my 'little voice' has never spoken to me as clearly as it did when I was searching for you."

"Why do you think that is?" Tanner said.

Alexa smiled at him. "We were meant to be together, to join forces, and soon the two of us will make Alvarado pay."

Tanner just stared at Alexa without speaking. He wanted to trust her and could use an ally, but he just didn't know what to think of her yet. One second, he was certain she was legit, and in the next instant, he would have doubts about her. Tanner lowered his gaze and went back to taping his end of the sheet closed.

"I found some papers," Alexa said. "They were in the closet and they had to do with the deaths of his wife and daughter. A lawsuit followed the fire; it was something about a faulty oven. This house and some money were left to him by his mother, she passed away not long after his family died, and… it looks like he just dropped out of life then."

Once they had the body wrapped, Alexa offered to help Tanner carry it up the basement stairs. Tanner assured her he could carry the bundle alone, and soon they were on the right side of the home, where they had decided to bury the body.

Tanner had made the hole deep. He and Alexa

lowered the corpse in the grave, covered it up, then sat an old wooden bench over the spot. It had begun to rain, but the forecast called for more of it to fall throughout the day, and to be heavy at times.

"I want to say a few words," Alexa said.

"Like what, a prayer?" Tanner said.

"Yes, it's one of my grandmother's favorites."

Alexa recited the prayer, in Spanish, as Tanner stood by silently. When she was finished, Tanner noticed that she wiped away a tear.

"Why are you crying?"

"This man, Ralph Harper, he suffered a great loss and then he just gave up. And this was a man who once embraced life. He was a racer, a competitor, and a winner; I was just thinking how terrible his loss must have been to cause him to just give up that way."

"Yes, but you lost far more than he did, and you never gave up."

"I had Rodrigo, my Papa… without his love… I may have turned inside and hidden myself away too."

Tanner reached over and touched her on the cheek. "Never give up; we all die soon enough."

Alexa took his hand. "Is that the Tanner motto?"

He smiled. "I guess it could be, and I also think we'd better get to work on our security precautions. Maybe we can finish before this rain gets too heavy."

He released her hand, but Alexa reached out and took it again. "Tanner."

"Yeah?"

"You're not what I expected."

"In what way?"

"You're… nicer than I'd thought you'd be, you know, for a hired killer."

"I chose my profession because I'm good at it, but I've

been so busy the last few months defending myself and helping out others that I haven't had a chance to take a real contract. Once Alvarado is dead and the past is behind me, I'm going to get back to basics, and that means taking a contract on a target. I am a killer, Alexa, and I won't apologize for it."

Alexa moved closer. "I wasn't criticizing you; it was actually the opposite."

Tanner was leaning in to kiss her when the sky opened up and the rain increased tenfold. Alexa screamed, then laughed, and while still holding Tanner's hand, she ran for the porch, while pulling him along.

Once they were beneath the cover of the roof, they stood together watching the rain, as flashes of lightning could be seen in the distance, followed by the rumble of thunder.

Alexa still gripped Tanner's hand, and as he looked out at the rain, he smiled.

21

WITH FRIENDS LIKE YOURS...

The huge coordinated raids on the Chemzonic chemical plants took place the next morning, and by noon, there were over thirty arrests in the United States and Mexico.

Jack Rockford's information was of incalculable value and it led Jake Garner to another source, one of Chemzonic's Vice-presidents. That Vice-President, the woman who Tanner had thought was losing her hair, also made a deal.

The woman looked relieved when Garner showed up at her home. She told him that the stress was killing her. Garner's superiors agreed to place her inside the witness protection program, and she revealed how Chemzonic had gotten in bed with the Alvarado Cartel.

It was simple. Chemzonic and the Alvarado Cartel were one and the same and had been since Chemzonic's founding in 2001.

The cartel owned several ancillary businesses as well, such as a chemical drum manufacturer and two trucking firms. They had also bribed or threatened over two dozen people to keep their secrets safe.

Within an hour of the raids, the killings began, as Alvarado tried to stop the damage and punish those who betrayed him. But all the key witnesses and their families had been placed on planes to unknown destinations before the raids began. The harm they caused to Alvarado's drug pipeline was epic.

The cartel could recover from it, eventually, and at great expense, but in the meantime, their customers in the western half of The United States would be supplied by others, such as Damián Sandoval, who was already making inroads into Alvarado's Mexico City territory.

～

MALENA STOOD BESIDE HER HUSBAND'S CHAIR AS THEY watched the press conference begin. Alvarado's office television took up most of one wall and was a hundred inches across diagonally. It made the people on the screen look life-size.

Special Agent Jake Garner was flanked by local agents from the FBI's Oklahoma City office, and he explained in general how the raids were carried out. When one of the reporters asked if their original informant had a code name, Garner stared into the cameras and smiled.

"His name is Tanner; at least, that's what he calls himself."

Alvarado's face went white, which lasted only a second before it turned crimson. He reached into the top drawer on his desk, removed a gun, and fired at the TV until the gun was empty and the television destroyed.

Malena knelt beside her husband's chair and took his

hand. "It has to be a coincidence; our Tanner couldn't be behind the raids on the plants... could he?"

Alvarado's breathing was ragged from the exertion caused by rage, but he calmed himself enough to speak.

"Rico said it best. Tanner is a devil. I believe it, and I believe something else."

"What, Alonso?"

"The devil is coming here. Tanner will make it past Martinez' men, past the multitude hunting him for the bounty, and he will be outside our walls. It is just a matter of time."

"Then we'll leave," Malena said, and even as the words left her lips, she knew her husband would never run.

Alvarado leaned over and kissed her. "I will stay, but you will go. I want you somewhere where you'll be safe."

"No Alonso, we stay together, and we work together, just as we did when we took over Mexico City."

Alvarado let out a sigh, and then nodded, as he drifted off into memory, the memory of his second rise to power.

MEXICO CITY 1998

MALENA ALVARADO SMILED WITH GENUINE PLEASURE AS SHE was greeted by her best friend, Ari Deleon. Ari was the wife of Juan Deleon, and Juan was Alonso Alvarado's best friend, and a former associate in the defunct Mercoto Cartel.

Ari and Juan's home was spectacular and sat on over fifty acres. Malena had been their frequent guest. That is, whenever she wasn't visiting her husband at the rehabilitative facility where he was recovering from his injuries, the ones he had received at the hands of Tanner Six.

Juan had been one of Alvarado's top men in Matamoras, one of his Knights as he liked to call them, another of his Knights had been Damián Sandoval, but Sandoval had staged a coup when Alonso had been injured, and Juan was forced to make a choice. Either he followed Sandoval, who was also a friend of his, or he would be killed.

Not a tough decision for most, and Juan had been no exception.

Although he did what he could for Malena and Alonso, they were considered persona non grata. If Sandoval knew that Juan was still in touch with Alvarado, he would have had him killed.

Ari looked out at the van Malena arrived in. "Why such a big boxy vehicle, Malena? Did you have to sell your cute little sports car?"

Malena kept the smile on her face, but it took effort. "Alonso and I are not peasants, Ari. The van is new. It was equipped for Alonso."

"For Alonso? I don't understand; I thought he was a cripple now."

The side door on the van slid open at the push of a button and revealed Alonso Alvarado. Alvarado was seated in a wheelchair, but he had a pair of crutches across his lap. The chair lowered to the ground mechanically, and although it seemed a struggle, Alonso stood with the aid of the crutches.

Ari's hand flew to her mouth and she told one of the servants to fetch her husband.

"What's wrong, Ari? You don't look happy to see me," Alvarado said.

Juan appeared. He had been Alvarado's best friend

since they were children and Alonso and Malena had named their only son after him, but when Juan saw Alvarado standing in his courtyard, he looked as upset as his wife.

"Good Lord, Alonso, are you trying to get all of us killed, man? Do you know what would happen if Sandoval knew you were here?"

Alonso smiled. "Aren't you going to invite me inside, Juan?"

"Yes, yes, get in here, but you cannot stay."

It took over a minute, but Alvarado made it up the stairs and into the house on his own power, but once inside, he fell into a thickly cushioned chair in the foyer.

The house was massive, and the foyer alone was as big as some homes. A chandelier hung from the thirty-foot ceiling, and above it, a skylight gave a view of the stars.

Juan looked distressed that Alvarado had sat. He stood before him pleading.

"It is so good to see you up and about, Alonso, but you really cannot stay here. We were taking a chance letting Malena visit us. Sandoval might accept her presence in his territory, but never yours."

Alvarado made a face of disgust. "Look at you! You've become Sandoval's dog. That traitorous bastard took advantage of my being attacked and killed Hector. Hector Mercoto was a friend, Juan, not just the head of our cartel, and the second he's dead you bow down to Sandoval. Tell me, do you lick the man's balls as well?"

Juan's arm shot out as he pointed toward the door. "Leave, or so help me I'll kill you myself and give you to Sandoval as a gift. You have no right to talk to me this way. Consider me a friend no more."

Alvarado held out one of the crutches and pointed its

tip at Juan's chest. "I stopped thinking of you as a friend the day you became Sandoval's lapdog."

After sliding down a lever on the side of it, Alvarado gripped the middle section of his right crutch and squeezed it as hard as his injured elbow joint allowed. It was enough, and the small charge at the tip of the crutch went off, to discharge six metal pellets.

Their impact staggered Juan. He looked down at his chest as six distinct red splotches appeared on his white shirt. The splotches expanded, met, and became one huge bloody stain. Juan looked up as if he were gazing through the skylight, then he fell forward and smacked the green marble floor like so much dead meat, which is what he was.

Ari had opened her mouth to scream when Malena jammed a knife in her back, then twisted it.

The scream died in Ari's lovely throat. She fell to her knees, where, after making a strangled cry, she collapsed beside her husband.

Juan's second-in-command walked over and stood to the side of Alonso's chair. He was named Cesare, and he too had known Alonso since they were children, but unlike Juan, he had never betrayed Alonso, he had simply played along and built alliances.

Most of Sandoval's people in Mexico City were still loyal to the old Mercoto Cartel, even if Sandoval had killed its leader. They would follow Alonso Alvarado, who they knew as a man of strength.

Cesare looked over at the two stunned servants, who in turn looked around for Ari and Juan's bodyguards. When they saw that the bodyguards weren't present, they knew the attack had been well planned.

Cesare smiled at the servants. "Bring in the belongings from the van. the Alvarado Cartel has begun."

22
TAKE A MESSAGE

After the press conference ended, Jake Garner was asked to join the head of the FBI's Oklahoma City Division. Her name was Jacqueline Thornton, and when Jake stepped into her office, he saw that she was not alone.

There was a man seated before her desk. He was about forty-five, short, and looked as if he could blend in anywhere. On the street, Jake wouldn't have sent him a second glance, but given where he was, he assumed the man was a spy.

Thornton stood and grabbed her laptop case from the desk. "Special Agent Jake Garner, this is Dan Matthews, and I will let you two gentlemen talk in private."

"Thank you, Jackie," Matthews said. He then stood and walked over to Jake to shake hands. "That was excellent work you did today. It'll cripple the Alvarado Cartel for months."

"Thank you, but it was all handed to me by our informant."

"Tanner, and don't bother with the code name business. I know that it's actually the name he goes by."

Garner studied Matthews more closely. "You're CIA, correct?"

Matthews smiled. "I was, but now I'm in the private sector. My employer is very interested in Tanner."

"And who would that employer be?"

"I'm not at liberty to say, and I'm hoping that you have a way to get in contact with Tanner."

"I don't. He contacted me at the office in New York City. We've had prior dealings, and I guess he trusts me enough to hand this information to me."

"Oh, I know all about those prior dealings, they occurred in the nation of Guambi."

"You and your employer are well informed. And if you want Tanner, that means one thing, you're looking for an assassin."

"No sir, we are looking for *the* assassin, and if he comes aboard, he will be paid well for his unique set of skills."

"As I said, I can't help you."

Matthews handed Jake a business card that had a handwritten phone number on it.

"If you somehow contact Tanner, please pass along our offer of employment and give him that number."

"As I said, I have no way to contact him."

Matthews grinned. "Yes, that is what you said. Goodbye Agent Garner, and again, congratulations on a job well done."

Matthews left the office, and Jake took one of two seats positioned in front of the desk. As Matthews suggested, he had lied. When Tanner contacted him, he also left Jake a way to contact him back via email.

Thornton returned to her office and smiled at Jake. "Dan Matthews is mysterious, don't you agree?"

"Yes, and how long have you known him?"

"We met at Dartmouth. He went into the Company, while I joined the Bureau."

"And who does he work for now?"

"I don't know, but I do know that when he went private three years ago, it was to take an offer from Burke."

"Conrad Burke, the defense contractor?"

"For his company, yes."

"I see, and thank you."

After Jake left Thornton's office, he went out and bought a cheap phone. Once he had it activated, he sent a message off to Tanner.

23

GOODBYE KISS

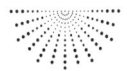

AT THE HOUSE IN OKLAHOMA CITY, ALEXA SHOWERED quickly then went downstairs to find Tanner awake, and a pot of coffee made. The preparations they put in place took longer than they thought they would, and they had worked until the early morning hours.

"Did you sleep well?" Tanner asked.

"I did, and you?"

"I got a few hours in, but I stayed awake after you went up and performed a second check on the work we did. It all seems good."

Alexa looked at the time on her phone. "I should be going soon if we're sticking to the plan, but I don't like that we're separating. And this trip you're sending me on, it feels like busy work."

"It's necessary; we'll need a place to go once it's known that we've been living here. While you're taking care of that, I'll be out making sure that the house gets discovered."

"But what if you don't show at the rendezvous point when I return?"

"I'll be there. But if I'm late, wait for me, and if you don't see me for hours... you'll know that someone is a million dollars richer and that I'm dead."

Alexa frowned at those words. "Don't die, Tanner, I have plans for you."

Tanner smiled. "That's good to know."

"I meant that I need you to help me kill Alvarado, well, it's the main reason."

"This plan will work, and by the end of the day we'll be somewhere safe, and we won't have a hit team on our trail."

"Are you certain that there is a hit team looking for you?"

"It's a logical assumption, and today we'll flush them out."

"All right, but when will we head to Mexico?"

"I'm not sure, but Tanner Six managed to talk sense into me in his emails. I need to come up with a plan for killing Alvarado and not just charge at the man like an enraged bull. Once I have that plan, we'll go to Mexico."

"Does that mean you trust me?"

"I do. It's why I'm sending you off alone to establish our new place. Do you remember where I told you to go?"

"Yes, and I'll be back as soon as I can, but what then?"

"We'll go see Tanner Six."

"He's close then?"

"Yes, he's very close to where you'll be going."

"I can't wait to meet him, and to tell my Papa about him. He'll be very interested in what both of you are like."

"Your Papa? That's the man that raised you, Rodrigo?"

"Yes, he saved my life, kept me safe, and I owe everything I am to him."

"I know what that's like. Tanner Six and I have a similar relationship."

"I see, and maybe someday you'll tell me about your history. After all, you know everything about me."

"Yes, maybe someday," Tanner said.

After a light breakfast and a final act of preparation, Tanner walked Alexa out to her van, where they stood by it, talking.

"If you get spotted or pursued while you're still close, give me a call," Tanner said.

"I can take care of myself," Alexa said.

"Yeah, I saw what you did to those bikers."

Alexa stared at Tanner. "I should get going."

"Um-hmm," Tanner said, as he stared back at her.

Their lips moved toward each other at the same time, and when they met, the kiss lasted for several seconds.

As they separated, each saw that the other one was smiling.

Alexa touched him on the cheek. "I'd better leave now, or we'll be off schedule."

"Right, and be safe, Alexa."

Alexa waved and smiled as she drove off, and Tanner smiled back at her. He hadn't lied when he said he trusted her, and yet, this was a final test, a verification of that trust.

Alexa knew his plans, knew where he'd be, and the extent of his weapons and ammo. If Tanner were attacked while she was absent, it would likely be by people she'd sent.

He shook his head ever so slightly, because he knew she was what she said she was, another victim of Alonso Alvarado, the man who was otherwise known as Martillo.

Tanner spent another hour at the house making sure that everything was in place, then he set off across the field behind the house and headed for the buildings in the distance.

He needed a car and would steal one, then, he would

hunt for those who were hunting him, and once he found them, he would lead them back to the house. The trap was set, and now it was time to spring it shut.

24
THAT'S EASY

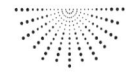

MEXICO

TANNER WASN'T THE ONLY ONE PREPARING FOR BATTLE. At the Alvarado compound, Alonso was watching as work was being done to fortify their defenses. He was on his crutches and standing near the fountain in the courtyard.

Shards of glass were being secured on top of the entire twenty-foot-high wall to make it even tougher to scale.

While that was being done, a second gate was in the process of being installed thirty yards out from the first one. It would allow a vehicle, even a large truck, to enter a walled-in area, where it would then be checked for explosives or stowaways. When the new gate was completed, any vehicle entering the compound would have to make its way through two separate checkpoints. The old gate was also being reinforced, so that nothing short of a tank could bust through it.

There were tents being erected beside the barracks, and as soon as the extra cots arrived, more men would be placed outside the compound to defend its walls in case of an attack.

Robert Martinez of Hexalcorp had suggested the changes, and Alvarado had agreed with every one of them. The ease with which Alexa penetrated their defenses made him realize he'd been taking his safety for granted.

Where before Alexa's visit, one man used to drive around the compound's wall three times a day, there would soon be a hundred men outside at all times, along with dogs and long-range snipers. There would also be new solar-powered lights installed out in the surrounding desert, and jeeps would regularly patrol the terrain. If Tanner couldn't make it to the walls, he certainly couldn't make it over them.

Martinez had been checking that the glass was being applied to every area of the wall. After climbing down a ladder, he walked over to speak with Alvarado.

"It's coming along fine, although I still say it's a mere precaution. My strike team is on the ground in Oklahoma. As soon as they get a bead on Tanner, well, he'll die."

Alvarado sighed wearily. "I don't even remember how many times I've heard those same words; all I know is that they've never come true."

"They will this time, Mr. Alvarado. You have my word. Do you think I would have pledged my life on that promise if I had even the slightest doubt?"

"I hear your words, the sincerity in them, but until Tanner is dead, they are just that, only words."

Martinez' phone rang, after answering it and speaking for a short time, he ended the call, and then fiddled with his phone until he brought up the sketch of Alexa. It was made from the description the young guard, Joaquin, had given to an artist. The likeness matched her well.

"This woman, you want her as well, yes?"

Alvarado gazed at the phone and a fire lit his eyes. "Yes. That bitch killed my brother-in-law."

"I just heard from my strike team leader, Steve Bennett. It looks like she's with Tanner. I guess the two of them are working together in Oklahoma."

The news perplexed Alvarado, and he looked at Martinez with a skeptical gaze. "Are you certain? That sounds unlikely."

"It hasn't been established as a fact yet, no, but my men have four witnesses who saw them together."

"Who are these witnesses?"

~

IN OKLAHOMA, SCAR, BRUISE, WOUND, AND ABRASION were all on their knees inside their motel room. Steve Bennett stood before them, looking down, with his men standing beside him.

With nothing else to do until Tanner resurfaced, Bennett and his men went to check out the motel where Tanner had killed the five men with a grenade.

While there, Hakeem had witnessed an argument between the motel's night clerk and a member of the local media.

The young reporter was sticking her finger in the clerk's face and telling him that he should go talk to the police, and that it was his civic duty. The clerk called the woman a second-rater and stuck out his own finger, his middle finger.

After Hakeem went over and talked to the clerk, he learned that he was looking to sell information. Minutes later, the man was a thousand dollars richer, and Bennett and his team knew about the Tin Horsemen Motorcycle

Club. The clerk knew the Horsemen because he used to live in Enid.

"Yeah, I work down here now but I come from Enid. That's up north a bit. Anyway, I know the four fools that were here when the grenade killed those gangsters. I see them all the time when I visit my sister. She lives right across the street from them, and Lordy if those crappy bikes of theirs don't make a racket."

Once they had the motorcycle club's address. Bennett called it all in to Martinez, who passed it along to Hexalcorp. Someone in the main office tracked Scar to a motel by way of his mother's credit card.

Bennett saw that the Tin Horsemen were scared, and an idea occurred to him, an idea similar to the one the deceased Georgie had. He would use the Horsemen as cannon fodder to help wear Tanner down.

"Get up, boys."

Scar had trouble standing, because every time he put pressure on either of his cut hands it hurt like hell, but he rose after Bruise gripped him by an elbow and tugged.

Bennett reached into his pocket and brought out a roll of money. Hexalcorp supplied the cash to him on every job. It usually went unused, but not today. The motel clerk had received a grand of it, and now Bennett handed each of the Tin Horsemen a hundred dollars.

"You four are on the payroll. I want you to ride around the city separately. The first one of you who spots Tanner or the woman will get five-hundred bucks, all right?"

The four fools smiled at each other, but Scar had a question. "We saw a third poster for some other dude. Will you pay if we find him too?"

"Hell yeah. Our employer wants that man as much as he wants Tanner, maybe even more so."

"Good," Scar said. "The guy looks familiar, but I can't remember where I've seen him."

"That's enough talk, get on your bikes and start looking."

Simms handed out cards to the boys. "If you find anything, call that number."

"But don't try to take Tanner or the others until after we arrive on the scene," Bennett said. "We, uh, we want to see you take them down."

"Us?" Bruise said, and a whistling sound accompanied the word due to his missing front tooth.

Roger Wilson smiled at the boys. "You're the Tin Horsemen, right? Hell, Tanner doesn't stand a chance against you guys."

Scar and his crew left, and Hakeem frowned at Bennett. "Steve, Tanner will tear through them like a chainsaw through tissue paper."

"Yeah, but while he's busy doing that, maybe one of us will get him lined up in our sights."

"Was there any news on Martinez' end?" Simms asked.

Bennett smiled. "Yeah, get this, they think Tanner was behind the raids on those drug companies. He's really got it in for Alvarado."

"I don't blame him," Hakeem said. "Alvarado is a dirtbag."

Bennett pointed at him. "Wrong. He's a client. We don't judge, remember? And you know as well as I do that the good guy/bad guy thing is bullshit. Look at us and the shit we've done for our country. To our fellow countrymen we're patriots and to our enemies we're the scum of the earth. All I know about Alvarado is that he can pay the bills. And oh yeah, he doesn't force people to buy drugs, he just supplies them."

Hakeem held up his hands in surrender. "I got it, but I still don't have to like the man."

"I don't either, but just like us, he is what he is."

"And Tanner, what's he?" Hakeem said.

Simms freed his gun from the shoulder holster beneath his jacket and pretended to take aim at a target.

"That's easy, Tanner is a dead man."

25

HELP WANTED – MUST BE WILLING TO KILL

After Tanner received Jake Garner's message about Dan Matthews, he called Matthews on the number given to him by Garner. After eight rings, Tanner was about to end the call when he heard a man answer the phone.

"Please hold while I activate security precautions."

The voice sounded bored, as if it spoke those same words often. Tanner guessed its owner was used to taking measures to ensure privacy. Tanner held on the line, and after a hiss of static, Matthews came back on.

"Only one man has this number, that is, unless he passed it along to another man."

"It's Tanner, and you're Matthews?"

"Dan Matthews. I want to talk to you about an employment opportunity."

"I work for myself. I don't hire on."

"That's understood, and if we reached an agreement, you would still be your own man. Still, my employer would like to be able to call on you when needed, at pay commensurate with your skill set, of course."

Tanner had two million dollars in an account after

being paid by Joe Pullo. To earn that money, he had killed scores of the Giacconi Family's enemies. It felt good knowing the money was there. He was through working for peanuts.

"If I took an assignment, the price would be one million dollars."

"Excuse me?" Matthews said.

"You heard me right."

"Yes, and I was told that you had a high opinion of yourself, I see that wasn't exaggerated."

"Conrad Burke can afford it."

"Ah, I see that Garner sniffed out my employer. Yes, Mr. Burke can afford it, but he could also hire six men for less."

"There aren't six men in the world that can do what I do."

"I don't know, Tanner; you'd be surprised at the talent pool out there. Unlike yourself, those men understand discipline and the chain of command because they've spent time in the armed forces."

"Fine, hire them, and when they fail, I'll want even more money."

Tanner heard an exasperated sigh come over the line. "It's my understanding that you're a marked man now. There's a two-million-dollar reward for you, dead or alive."

"*Two* million? Hmm, Alonso Alvarado is getting nervous."

"The point is, Tanner, you may not live long enough to take a contract."

"Tell Burke my terms, one million a contract, but I get to refuse any offers made."

"We also have terms."

"Such as?"

"This offer is only valid if you're successful in killing Alvarado, which, of course, is impossible. The man is locked away inside that desert fortress and our satellite surveillance reveals that he's fortifying his defenses. By the way, if you're going after Alvarado, you're headed the wrong way."

"I have business north before I head south."

"I believe you. You're not the type to hide or run, I'll give you that much."

"I get the impression that recruiting me wasn't your idea?"

"You're correct. However, you have an advocate within our organization and Mr. Burke agrees with them, at least for now."

"What's the name of this advocate?"

"I'm not at liberty to say."

"Can I assume that I'm not the first man you've approached to take this job?"

"You're correct again. Three men went after a certain target and two of the men have disappeared."

"What about the third?"

"His body was found yesterday."

"Is the target foreign or domestic?"

"An American living abroad, but he's a very dangerous man."

"It sounds interesting, and I do like a challenge, although, once I kill Alvarado, I'll be taking some serious down time. If you still need me after that, let me know."

"Down time? I don't think you understand. The man I'm talking about should have been put in his grave weeks ago."

"That's not my problem. If you still need help in a month or so, I'll think about it."

"You'll think—goddamn it! I'll talk Burke out of using

you somehow, and Alvarado will probably kill you anyway."

"What's got you so upset, Matthews? Is it my lack of discipline or the fact that I don't give a damn about your problem?"

"It's not *my* problem, Tanner, this affects the world."

Tanner had been smirking into the phone, but Matthews's words intrigued him.

"What are we talking about here, a terrorist?"

"This is a man who funds terrorists, chiefly because they further his own agenda."

"All right, but there's something I don't get. Why is Burke in the assassination business? The government has its own killers and black ops to do this sort of work."

"Yes, and they've all failed before we were ever consulted. The government outsources many areas to us; Mr. Burke was hoping to expand into this arena as well. However, we've proven as ineffective as the government in this case."

"It sounds interesting, but my focus is on killing Alonso Alvarado; until that's done, nothing else matters."

"I understand that, and… I can help you."

"How?"

"As I said before, we have the Alvarado compound under satellite surveillance. I'll forward that to Garner and then he can forward it to you."

"That would be helpful. I take back what I was thinking about you, Matthews."

Matthews chuckled. "You kill Alvarado, Tanner, and I'll believe you're as good as you think you are."

"It's a deal," Tanner said, then he ended the call.

26

METER READER

After speaking with Dan Matthews, Tanner had driven around the city for hours.

When he spotted the group of eight men gathered together in the side parking lot of a bar, he was almost certain he had found what he was looking for.

The men all had the carriage of soldiers and were likely a group of mercenaries looking to cash in on the bounty placed on his head. They appeared to be organized, but they were not the men that Tanner Six had warned him about. Those men would not stand around a public parking lot to make their plans. Those men would be secreted somewhere just waiting for him to stick his head up so they could chop it off.

Still, he could use this group to make the other group show themselves, and once they did so, he would be the one doing the chopping.

~

While shopping with Alexa the day before, Tanner had bought a set of green work clothes, along with a clipboard and calculator.

He was wearing those clothes, and after donning a plain black baseball cap and a pair of sunglasses, Tanner left the car and began working his way closer to the men inside the parking lot.

He stopped at each business he came to and went around to the gas meter. If the meter were an older model, Tanner pretended to copy down the numbers he read onto the clipboard. If the gas meter was electronic, he held the calculator against it, as if it were a device to gather data from the meter.

He had used the ploy once before when he'd only had a clipboard, and his target at the time, a perceptive man who was in hiding, made him as a phony and slipped away. He eventually killed the man, as a Tanner never failed to fulfill a contract, but the lesson was learned, and the mistake would never be repeated.

When he was checking the meter on the dry cleaners that sat next to the bar's parking lot, the men stopped talking for a moment as they looked over at him. They soon dismissed him as simply a man doing his job and resumed making their plans.

The largest of the men, a bearded giant wearing faded overalls, spoke to the others.

"Two million, man, you know whoever wants this Tanner really wants him when they're willing to pay that much now."

One of the other men smiled. "You know what we should do if we bag him. We should keep quiet and wait until the price goes higher."

"Screw that," said another man who wore a goatee. "Once we get him, I'm cashing in and heading to Vegas."

The other men laughed, then the big one opened up a paper map. From what Tanner gathered as he walked past them to check the bar's meter, they were dividing the city up into grids to search. That was good, it meant that they would be separating into smaller groups and make themselves more vulnerable.

Tanner pretended to check the meters up and down each side of the block while the men made their plans. When the eight men separated into four sets of two, he decided to go with goatee and his partner, a skinny guy with sunburned skin. That was when Tanner noticed that all the men had good tans, and he wondered where they were from. Wherever it was, they should have stayed there.

It seemed Matthews was right. His bounty had been doubled to two million dollars. That was a good sign; it meant that Alvarado was worried.

Alvarado must have seen the drawing of him as well as the old mugshot, but whether he realized that he was Cody Parker, Tanner didn't know. He had only been sixteen when Alvarado killed his family and left him for dead, and as he had believed Alvarado long dead, Alvarado must have believed likewise about him.

If Alvarado didn't realize that Tanner and Cody Parker were one and the same, Tanner would reveal it to the man before he killed him. Alvarado had murdered Tanner's family, and he would finally pay for that act.

Alexa had suffered too, even more so than Tanner had, given how young she was at the time. He could only imagine the damage that such a horrific experience must have caused the child she once was.

Tanner wondered about her briefly. Was she off doing as he asked her to do, or was everything she'd told him a lie and she had some unknown agenda? Tanner hoped she would pass her final test, because if she didn't, he'd have to kill her.

He followed behind Goatee and his partner in his stolen car as they drove off in a silver Toyota pickup. The license plate on the rear of the truck told Tanner that the men were from Arizona. That answered Tanner's earlier question about where the men had come from.

After he thought enough time had passed to allow the other groups to travel far enough away, he decided to lure Goatee and Sunburn back to the house where he and Alexa had been staying.

~

While Tanner was busy looking for someone to lead into their trap, Alexa had been driving to the northeastern portion of Oklahoma to a lake that had cabins for rent.

Tanner had told her of a place he stayed at before and knew to be secluded. It was the off-season and empty cabins would be plentiful.

Alexa was to get a cabin, stock it with food, then return to Oklahoma City for Tanner. It was a six-hour round trip with the shopping included. She felt as if he was trying to keep her out of harm's way by sending her off on an errand.

Then again, when she arrived at the lake, she saw what Tanner had meant. No one would think of looking for them in such a picturesque environment. And as half of a vacationing couple, Tanner would be even less conspicuous.

Alexa took a cabin that sat among a group of three. The other two appeared empty, as no vehicles were parked outside their doors. She then followed the directions of the woman who had rented her the cabin and shopped at a local supermarket.

She had rented the cabin with the story that her husband would be joining her there later for a vacation break. When Alexa first entered the cabin and saw that it contained only one bed, she smiled.

Tanner must have known that there was only one bed per cabin. It would serve him right if she made him sleep on the sofa. That was unlikely, she knew, because she wanted him as much as he wanted her.

When she returned from the market, she saw with a small bit of irritation that they did have a neighbor in one of the other cabins. It irked Alexa because it meant they would have to be more on guard. However, the woman seemed friendly enough, and like Alexa, her partner would be joining her later that day.

"Oh yeah, Bob and I come here every year about this time. We love it here."

"Is it quiet? My husband likes his privacy."

"Oh honey, it's full of quiet, and you don't have to worry about Bob and me, we'll spend most of our time out on the lake fishing."

Alexa said goodbye to the woman, and with all the preparations done, she locked up the cabin, climbed into her van, and headed back to Oklahoma City to meet up with Tanner.

As she drove along, she thought about her Papa Rodrigo, and Emilio, and wondered how they were doing. She never once realized she was being followed by Spenser Hawke, or that her friendly neighbor in the other cabin had actually been Amy.

Alexa drove on, unaware that she was leading Spenser straight to Tanner's location.

27

SPILLED BLOOD

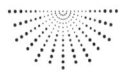

TANNER FOLLOWED THE TWO MERCENARIES AND SAW THEM pull into the parking lot of a donut shop. The place was only about three miles away from the house he wanted to lure them to, so he decided to make his move.

Goatee ran inside and came out a few minutes later with two cups of coffee, one of which he handed to Sunburn.

Tanner drove into the lot and parked near them, then got out of the car and went inside the donut shop. He had replaced the green work shirt with a black sweatshirt and had taken off the cap and sunglasses.

As Goatee began backing his pickup out of its parking space, Tanner thought he had been too subtle about things. But then, out of the corner of his eye, he saw the other man, Sunburn, spill coffee on himself and point his way.

Goatee had brought the car to a stop in such a manner that he was blocking the entrance to the lot, while he and the other man talked about Tanner. When the driver of a car trying to enter the parking lot blew her horn, Tanner saw Goatee send her an apologetic wave and drive over to park against a fence.

Here's where things could get tricky, Tanner thought.

If the men were stupid, they would try to kill him right there in the parking lot. However, if they had any sense at all, they would call in the troops, the other six men that had been with them.

Tanner bought two donuts, and as he left the shop, he pretended to be reaching into the bag for one. He wasn't reaching into the bag for a donut, but rather, he was using the bag to conceal the small gun he held. If Goatee and Sunburn made a move, he would shoot at them right through the bag. Fortunately, he saw that Sunburn was on the phone and talking rapidly. That was good, and it got better when the men began following him back to the house.

Tanner drove calmly and pretended not to know they were there until he was at the last traffic light before reaching the house. That was when he adjusted his rearview mirror and appeared to notice the men in the pickup, who were in the next lane behind a car.

Goatee and Sunburn immediately looked elsewhere, and when the light changed, Tanner made a left and sped off down the quiet road where the house was located. Moments later, as he approached the entrance to the property, Tanner slowed, then made a hard right into the graveled driveway.

Goatee and his friend were feeling the adrenaline and were on the hunt, and as Tanner hoped they would, they threw caution to the wind and raced after him. As they did so, Sunburn was shouting into his phone and giving the other men their location.

As Tanner neared the parking area at the front of the

home, he headed left toward the wide field, even as Goatee and Sunburn entered the graveled driveway.

When he had gone far enough to the left, Tanner made a sharp right while pulling up on the parking break. The car shuddered to a halt after having turned around 180 degrees.

Tanner leapt out. He fired two rounds from a Mossberg tactical shotgun into the front grill of the pickup truck. Goatee lost control, sideswiped Tanner's stolen car, and plowed right into a large oak tree.

Tanner fired another shot. He wasn't shooting to kill, and so he just flattened a rear tire. Goatee and Sunburn staggered out of the driver's side and stood looking about for a second.

Tanner let out an exasperated breath. He was trying to let the two idiots live, but they were making it so easy to kill them.

Tanner fired a shot over their heads and the men ducked down. When they returned fire, the fools did so by standing up and steadying their arms on top of the pickup truck's roof, thus leaving their midsections exposed through the vehicle's window glass.

Every shot they made was either wide or too high. The only thing they managed to hit was a tire and a branch on a small tree near the house. Tanner wondered if they ever practiced their shooting.

He sighed again and fought the urge to shoot them both dead. Instead, he took aim at Goatee and placed a round on the outer part of his left shoulder, a shot that barely grazed him.

Goatee howled, more from fear than pain, then finally, he and Sunburn headed into the trees to make their way back out to the road.

Tanner followed them until he was certain they were

leaving, then ran back to the house, went to the refrigerator, and removed a jar.

The jar contained blood, his and Alexa's which they had taken from each other that morning.

Tanner returned outside where he emptied nearly half the jar beside the stolen car, before using the other half to leave a trail of blood from the car, up the porch stairs, and into the house.

He had cut the side of his hand earlier, before leaving, and let it drip blood up the stairs inside the house. In the bathroom, there were bloodstained towels and an empty box of gauze that spoke of someone attempting to treat a serious wound.

Anyone finding the blood trail would think him wounded and hiding within the house, and with a two-million-dollar price tag on his head, they likely wouldn't leave until they had torn the place apart. That would take time and draw his pursuers in, and ultimately, the team hunting him for Alvarado would come to the house. Once revealed and identified, they could be eliminated.

After leaving the house, Tanner checked the location of the two men, and saw them out on the road. They were talking to two of their partners who had just arrived on the scene.

While they were planning their next move, Tanner bolted across the field at the home's rear, crossed the other road, and climbed over the fence, to walk behind a bowling alley. When he saw Alexa's van, he realized he was looking forward to seeing her. She greeted him with a smile as she opened the rear doors.

There was a card table in the back of the van with a trio of laptops on it. Alexa sat in front of the table in a folding chair. Tanner took the one beside her, as she pointed at the laptops.

"Every camera is working perfectly except for two of them, and I saw how you handled those men at the house."

"You mean the idiots? Neither one could shoot straight and the one with the goatee ran his truck into a tree and nearly killed them both."

Alexa grinned. "I saw that. You're even deadly when you're not trying to be. I rented the cabin, and that lake looks beautiful."

"Any problems?"

"No, but we will have neighbors in a nearby cabin."

"Neighbors? More than one?"

"Yes, a woman with dark hair, but I haven't met her husband."

"I've been told that a woman named Ariana O'Grady is hunting for me, and that she has dark hair. How old was the woman?"

Alexa recalled Amy and shrugged with one shoulder. "Not old or young, maybe mid-thirties, and she was beautiful."

"Hmm, she sounds too old and too good looking to fit the description I was given of Ariana. Still, we'll keep an eye out for her since we'll soon have the people hunting me searching that house."

Alexa pointed at the middle laptop. "It's already started."

Tanner looked and saw that two of Goatee's friends had found the blood trail that led into the house.

"That's a start, and word will spread about the house, human nature will see to that."

Alexa hit several keys on the laptop and took still photos of the mercenaries, then, she sent them to the printer that was on the floor beneath the table.

Tanner looked at the photos. "This is good work, but we don't have to worry about most of these people. If I had to guess, I'd say we're looking for a team of three or four men."

"If they are as good as you say, they may show at the house very soon."

Tanner shook his head. "Actually, I would expect them to be last. They'll let everyone else do all the searching and then come in at the end to verify I'm really not in there."

"But wouldn't they fear that someone would find you first?"

"No, because if that happened, they would just kill whoever had me and take me from them. These are men who will fear no one, because they've never met anyone better than they are."

Alexa turned in her seat and studied him. "But you're better than they are, aren't you?"

"Yes."

Alexa leaned in and kissed him. "I find confidence very sexy. I also missed you while I was off on my errand."

"I assume there's no one back in Mexico waiting for you, or is there?"

"No, my recent lifestyle doesn't offer many dating opportunities."

"Is this your first time in the US?"

"I went to college in Texas, but I dropped out after two years because I knew I could learn more on my own."

"Have you ever been to Hawaii?"

"No."

"When this is over and Alvarado is dead, you and I will go there. I need some serious down time, and I'm sure you do too."

Alexa smiled. "That sounds like a plan; it also sounds like you finally trust me."

"I do trust you, Alexa, and together we'll kill Alvarado."

A flurry of movement on the right-hand laptop screen caught Tanner's eye and he pointed at it.

"They look familiar."

It was the Tin Horsemen. They had followed the last two mercenaries of the group to the house and were being told to leave by the other mercs who were already there.

There was no sound, only video, but it looked like two of the mercenaries wanted to use the Horsemen as backup. The mercenaries' leader, the bearded giant in the overalls, disagreed, and he was telling the Tin Horsemen to go away.

~

Bruise sent the big man the finger as the Tin Horsemen parked their bikes across the road from the house, and next to the slope that led down to the stream. The water was higher and moving faster than it had been before the heavy rain of the previous night. Bruise cursed as his boot became covered in the slick mud at the side of the road.

Scar took out his phone, which it hurt him to grip with his injured hand. After two rings, he heard the voice of Hexalcorp's strike team leader, Steve Bennett.

"Talk to me."

"There's some guys that say they have Tanner trapped in a house."

"Give me the address."

Scar gave it to him and then asked Bennett what he wanted them to do.

"Just keep watch. Once Tanner kills those men, try to follow him, we're on our way."

"Tanner might have run out of luck. There's a whole

bunch of guys here, and they say that Tanner lost a lot of blood when their friends shot him."

"Really? That's interesting, but do like I said and keep watch."

"How soon can you get here?"

"We're not coming there, but we'll be nearby, just keep watch and call me when something happens."

"Okay," Scar said.

∽

Bennett put his phone away as he and his men were headed out the door. "Our four boys say that Tanner is wounded and holed up in a house."

Hakeem smiled. "That sounds like one of Tanner's traps."

"Exactly, which is why we'll be staying back and watching what happens."

"You think the house is booby trapped?"

Bennett climbed behind the wheel of a large black Chevy pickup. The vehicle came from Hexalcorp's Oklahoma office. It had been delivered to them at the airport, complete with weapons and other equipment.

"I don't know if Tanner booby trapped the house, but I do know one thing about Tanner."

"What's that?" Wilson said.

"He never runs out of ways to kill you."

28

CHESS MOVES

Like Bennett, Spenser didn't believe that Tanner was inside the house in Oklahoma City. He stayed at the lake with Amy. They were together outside the cabin that Alexa had rented, as Spenser worked on picking the lock on the rear door.

Amy was looking down at the drawing of Alexa that declared she was wanted dead or alive. Spenser had printed out a copy of it before leaving his house.

"So, they're both wanted?"

"Yes, and Tanner is now worth two million."

Amy's mouth formed into an O. "That's a lot of money, Spenser."

"Tell me about it," he said, and then he laughed.

"What's funny?"

"This stupid lock; it's broken. We could have just walked right in. I'll be sure to check the lock on our own door when we get back."

Spenser opened the door and they entered. They went about the cabin looking over the things that Alexa had bought at the market.

Amy called from the bedroom as Spenser checked out the kitchen. "There's a duffel bag on the closet floor. Should I look through it?"

"Yes, but be careful to put things back as you found them," Spenser said, "We don't want to tip her off that someone's been here."

When they were through with their search, Spenser and Amy left the way they had entered and returned to their own cabin.

"What now?" Amy asked.

"Now we wait for them to come here."

Amy gazed about. "I'm nervous. This isn't like one of your cases."

"No, it's not, and you can still leave. I'd feel better if I knew you were somewhere safe and completely out of the line of fire."

Amy hugged him. "No, I'm with you no matter what, remember?"

"I do, and when this is over, we'll take that trip to New Orleans, count on it."

Amy hugged Spenser tighter. She didn't want to say it aloud, but she was getting a bad feeling.

∾

AT THE HOUSE IN OKLAHOMA CITY, THE TIN HORSEMEN watched as five of the mercenaries who had been inside the house came out and talked to the men who were guarding the entrance to the driveway.

Three other groups of bounty hunters had shown up. It was Bennett's doing. He wanted as many people as possible searching that house before he and his team stepped a foot inside it. If there were traps, he preferred to let someone else get caught in them.

One of the new arrivals called over to the mercenaries who had been inside the house.

"Did you get him? Did you get Tanner?"

The big man who led the mercenaries held up several receipts. "We searched the whole damn house and couldn't find Tanner, but these receipts make me think the place might be booby trapped. There's enough supplies on these slips to build a dozen pipe bombs, and we spotted wire scraps and cut pieces of pipe on a table in the basement. If Tanner is hiding in there somewhere, I think he'll blow up the first man that finds him."

Two of the men were professional bounty hunters from Texas. The two stalked over and spoke to the mercenaries.

"We're going in. If you don't want trouble, don't try to stop us."

"Go on in, but if you get an arm blown off don't come crying to me."

The two men pushed by them, and the others who had been standing around followed them down the driveway.

~

BENNETT HAD PARKED ON THE SIDE OF THE ROAD NOT VERY far from the house. Scar had just called to tell him what was happening. When the call ended, Bennett told his men what Scar had relayed to him.

"It looks like a bunch of losers are tearing that house apart looking for Tanner."

"What if he's really in there, could he hide from them?" Hakeem said.

"If I gave you a day to build a hiding place inside a house do you think you could do it?"

Hakeem considered Bennett's question and then

nodded. "Yeah, all I would really need to do is build a false wall with a hidden latch."

"Or you could hide under the floorboards, or above the basement ceiling, or even inside a large piece of furniture," Bennett said.

Simms chuckled. "If we can think of that, so will those yahoos inside the house who are looking for Tanner. I bet they tear that place apart."

"Yeah," Bennett said. "And that's why I don't think Tanner is in that house. I think this is all a trick to flush us out."

"What's that mean?" Wilson said.

Bennett's phone rang. He grabbed it from its charger on the dashboard and looked at the caller ID. "It's Martinez."

As soon as Bennett answered the phone, Martinez spoke. "Give me some good news that I can tell the client."

"Take this with a grain of salt, but it looks like Tanner might be injured and holed up in a house here."

"If that's the case, why aren't you going in there after him?"

"Because I'm not convinced he's in there. I think he's somewhere doing just what we're doing, he's sitting back and watching the show."

"What would be the point of that?"

"I think he's trying to draw us out."

"What? How would he even know you're after him?"

"He doesn't know our names, but he knows that Alvarado will send someone. I think that this is his way of smoking us out."

"Ah, but that would mean he'd have to be watching from somewhere close, no?"

"My guess is that he has cameras strung up around the property."

"This is like a chess match. So what's your next move?"

"For now, we'll just wait and see what develops; as the saying goes, only fools rush in."

"Steve, you've got to get this bastard. You know what it will mean for all of us if you fail."

"Alvarado would really kill you?"

"If he didn't, that wife of his would, she's as scary as he is."

"Don't worry, Martinez, Tanner's good, but we're better."

"I hear you, and I have complete faith in you. Call me when you have him."

Bennett ended the call and saw that his men were all looking around, as if Tanner were lurking in the bushes.

"Chill, guys. Wherever Tanner is, he's waiting for us to show at the house, and once we do, we'll have him."

"How do you figure that?" Simms asked.

"I'll walk in there with you and Wilson after Hakeem gets into position with a sniper rifle. We'll wait for Tanner to show himself. When he does, while thinking that he has the upper hand, Hakeem will surprise him with a bullet to the head. He can't hide from a night vision scope."

Hakeem laughed. "We used that same trick in Iraq three times. Yeah, it should work, but Steve, what about the woman he's with?"

"What about her? She'll die just like Tanner."

"Martinez said that she made it inside Alvarado's compound on her own. Maybe we shouldn't underestimate her."

"We won't, but what can she do to us?"

Wilson held aloft the drawing of Alexa. "If she's as hot as this picture, I can think of a few things I'd like her to do to me."

The men all laughed along with Wilson. They were completely unaware that Tanner was watching them.

29

I SEE YOU

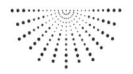

Bennett was right when he guessed that Tanner had cameras strung up around the home's property, but Tanner and Alexa had also placed outdoor cameras up in trees and attached to light poles in the surrounding area.

There were nearly thirty cameras in use, although two of them weren't operating properly. Tanner and Alexa had worked into the early morning hours in the pouring rain while getting everything done; now it was paying off.

The cameras even had night vision capability. Tanner Six had suggested the idea, but Alexa had shown Tanner how to install them.

A trained thief, Alexa knew about surveillance equipment. She had connected the cameras wirelessly to a trio of laptops, and now the rear of her van looked like a small security office.

Tanner had zoomed in on Bennett and Wilson, who were seated in the front of the vehicle. He had marked them as likely candidates for the men hunting him for Alvarado, but when Wilson held aloft the drawing of Alexa, he knew for certain they were the ones.

"That's them?" Alexa said.

"I think it's a safe bet," Tanner said. "They're the only ones staying back. I think they're just waiting to see what develops."

"How do you want to handle this?" Alexa asked. "It looks like there are four men in that truck."

"We'll wait along with them, and when they finally make their move, we'll make ours. Alvarado hired them, but I want to know who they really work for."

"Waiting for them to make the first move, is that your whole plan, or do you have something specific in mind?"

Tanner reached over to grab his drag bag from the floor. A "drag bag" is the term snipers coined for a tactical rifle case. Tanner opened the case and removed his weapon, a Barrett M82A1 sniper rifle.

"This is all the plan I'll need."

~

WHILE SITTING ACROSS FROM ALVARADO IN THE CARTEL leader's office, Martinez told Alvarado that Tanner was believed to be wounded and hiding inside a house. Alvarado gave him a skeptical look.

"Who wounded him?"

"That's unknown, but he was identified, that means he's still in the same area as my team. It's just a matter of time until they get him."

Alvarado sighed. "One of my men, Rico Nazario, he thinks that Tanner is a devil. I agree with him. If your men are as good as you think they are, they'll stay out of that house. Tanner recently used gas to kill over a hundred men inside a building."

Martinez leaned back in his seat and crossed his legs. It was a move that he hoped would look confident, although, he was growing nervous. He had thought Tanner would be dead already.

"My men are aware of Tanner's tactics. They've been fully briefed, and they won't act until they're sure it's the right move."

Alvarado looked out through the patio doors. "I should put more men on the perimeter," he muttered.

"Sir, Tanner will never make it this far, trust me."

Alvarado stared at Martinez for several seconds. "How many men are still inside the compound?"

"A little over sixty at any given time, why?"

"Send half of them outside and extend the perimeter guard."

"That's really unnecessary."

"Just do it, as you said earlier, if Tanner can't make it to the wall, he won't make it over the wall."

Martinez rose to his feet. "I'll take care of that right away."

After Martinez left the room, Alvarado stared off into space.

"He's coming here, I can feel it."

30

TRUST

By nightfall, over a dozen men and women had been inside the home looking for Tanner. They had torn up floorboards, knocked holes in walls, and demolished several pieces of furniture.

When it became apparent that the home wasn't booby trapped, Bennett made a call and told Scar, Bruise, Wound, and Abrasion to go check out the house. They did so, and when they finished, Bennett gave them directions to his location.

Hakeem and Simms leaned over Bennett's shoulders as he scrolled through Scar's phone. They were looking at pictures Scar had taken inside the home and were interested in the photo of the huge bloodstain Tanner had left outside, near the car he had stolen.

"If that's real and Tanner is out there somewhere wounded, he's lost a lot of blood," Hakeem said.

"It's not real," Bennett said. "It was just bait."

Scar yawned. "We're heading back to our motel if you don't need us anymore."

"Yeah, you boys do that, but one more thing, was the house empty when you left?"

"Oh yeah, and it's too dark to see where you're going in there because somebody tore apart the wall where the circuit breakers were. They thought Tanner might be hiding behind there, and Wound almost fell into one of the holes that were made in the floors."

Wilson spoke up. "Hey, tell me something, when did you guys come up with these nicknames of yours, Scar, Wound, Bruise, and… what's the other guy's name, Contusion?"

"It's Abrasion," Abrasion said. "We made the names up in the third grade and they just stuck."

"Third grade, huh? That explains a lot," Wilson said, and Scar and the other Tin Horsemen rode away.

Bennett watched them go, then he spoke to his men.

"All right boys; let's get to work."

∽

At the van, Alexa pointed at the monitor where Bennett and his men were on camera.

"They're on the move."

Tanner checked the other cameras and saw no sign of Scar and his followers. "It looks like the bikers have left the area."

"If these men are as elite as you think they are, I'm surprised they would be working with those four fools."

"I'm sure they were just using them."

They followed the progress of Bennett's truck, which was rolling along slowly with its lights off. When it stopped, it was a hundred yards from the house, and Bennett and his men climbed out. The camera in that area was acting up; Alexa couldn't get it to switch to night vision mode.

"Damn it, all I see are four shapes," she said.

Tanner pointed at the screen. "Yeah, but look at the silhouette on that one. It looks like I won't be the only one with a rifle, and you can bet that his night vision scope will work better than our camera."

Alexa grabbed a black hoodie and put it on. "I'll go after him and eliminate the threat."

"That's dangerous, Alexa. What if he sees you first?"

"I'm not a Tanner, but I've been killing Alvarado's men for months. Most of that killing was done in the dark, guerilla-style. I'll kill that man before he even knows he's dead. Trust me."

"If you don't kill him, he'll try to kill me when I confront the others."

"I'm not the type of woman that needs saving, Tanner. When I say I'll do something, I'll do it. I'll kill that man."

Tanner looked away from Alexa and stared at the monitor. Bennett, Simms, and Wilson were back in the pickup and driving toward the house, while Hakeem was on foot and carrying his rifle.

"He just broke off from the others and is headed this way. Go kill him."

Alexa smiled, gave Tanner a soulful kiss, and left the van with a knife gripped in her right hand.

"Take a gun with you," Tanner said.

Alexa called back to him over her shoulder. "I'm better with a blade."

Tanner watched her from the rear doors of the van as she disappeared into the night.

He trusted Alexa, and now he would find out just how good she was.

Tanner closed the doors, started the van, and headed toward the house.

31

IT'S A BLAST

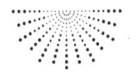

HAKEEM TOOK POSITION AT THE RIGHT SIDE OF THE OLD shed that looked as if it would fall over if a hard breeze came along.

The ground there was slightly elevated from the land the house sat on, so Hakeem settled onto his belly on the grass, then extended his rifle's fold-down bipod for extra stability. He had been in position for nearly a minute when he saw Bennett, Simms, and Wilson enter the moonlit area in front of the house.

He used the night vision scope to search for Tanner, but still didn't spot him until he appeared at the edge of the trees. When he saw that Tanner had a rifle as well, he tensed up. He then became even more nervous when he realized he was no longer alone.

AFTER ALEXA HAD LEFT THAT MORNING, TANNER HAD cleared a path through the trees by removing dead leaves and anything else that would crunch underfoot. He used that path to move toward the house in a crouch. To his surprise, Bennett was talking to him. Actually, Bennett was looking up at the old, rusted flagpole in the yard as he spoke, because he had spotted one of the cameras perched up there.

"My name is Bennett, Tanner. If you're half the man I think you are, you'll show yourself. As you can see, there's three of us, but our guns are holstered. I'm here to offer you a deal from Alonso Alvarado. He says if you give him the woman, he'll take the price off your head. The bitch killed his friend and so he wants her more than he wants you."

Only silence answered Bennett's lies. He looked over at Simms, and Simms shrugged.

"I guess he's not here."

"Wrong," Tanner said, as he stepped out of the trees to the left of the house. He was holding the long sniper rifle in both hands. It was pointed toward the men but held at waist level.

Bennett smiled at him, and as Tanner watched, all three men moved slowly to their right, until they were several feet from where they had been standing.

Tanner smiled back at Bennett, as he caught the repeated flash of reflected moonlight coming from the area by the shed.

If Bennett's man were the professional that Tanner assumed he'd be, he wouldn't be broadcasting his position that way. It was Alexa. He was certain of it. It was her way of signaling that she had made her kill.

"You moved to the right to get out of the line of fire, which would mean that your man with the rifle is out by that old shed in the field."

The smile left Bennett's face and he turned his head to glance toward the shed, before looking back at Tanner.

"If you know about Hakeem... then why did you show yourself?"

"Because Hakeem is dead," Tanner said. "The woman killed him."

"Bullshit!" Bennett said, and he raised a fist in the air to signal Hakeem to fire.

The first round passed only inches from Tanner's head. He actually saw it. It was a mangled piece of metal that tumbled end over end.

The round had entered Simms' back, took a wicked ricochet off two ribs, and exited below Simms' breastbone with most of its force spent.

Before Bennett knew what was happening, Wilson was down as well, as the second round all but decapitated him.

Bennett dove for cover, but Tanner brought his rifle up and took a shot without aiming through the scope. He hit Bennett while the man was still in midair. Bennett slammed into the ground like a loose sack of grain. Tanner's round had hit home and had entered Bennett's chest near its center.

Tanner walked over and stared down at him. "Who do you really work for?"

Bennett didn't answer; he rolled over onto his stomach and spat up blood. That's when Tanner saw that his shot had exited out of Bennett's back and left a ragged hole. The man was done for.

Bennett moaned, but his hands were busy beneath him, and Tanner wondered if the man had a hidden weapon. Tanner pushed him onto his back and saw that Bennett was smiling. He then noticed the grenade pin in Bennett's hand, as moonlight shone on it.

Tanner dived behind a nearby oak tree just as the grenade went off.

The pain was instant, agonizing, and it was coming

from his left calf. When Tanner looked down, he saw something sticking out of his pant leg that looked like a giant splinter.

"Tanner!" Alexa called.

She was running across the field while carrying Hakeem's sniper rifle. When she came to what was left of Steve Bennett, she had to pause to fight back the bile threatening to rise in her throat. When she spotted Tanner behind the tree, she set down the rifle and ran to him.

Tanner was sitting up and carefully tearing away the fabric around his calf. When the wound was revealed, he saw that it was part of the tree embedded in the muscle of his lower left leg, with the bark side facing down. When he placed his hand on the dagger-like chunk of wood, Alexa stopped him from pulling it free.

"Don't! Not here. We'll remove it in the van where I can treat the wound, but can you walk?"

Tanner stood and found that he limped, but the leg held his weight.

After wincing from the pain, he sent Alexa a smile. "That was damn fine shooting, but I thought you said you were better with blades."

"I am better with blades, but I'm also a good shot. Now lean on me and tell me where you left the van."

"It's through the trees on the left and parked near the stream."

They traveled back to the van slowly along the same path Tanner had taken on his way in. Tanner told Alexa to stand still before they left the cover of the trees, then he listened for any sounds that shouldn't be there.

There were none that he could discern, only the sound of the fast-flowing stream and the soft sound of traffic drifting in from the highway in the distance. Tanner nodded at Alexa, and they crossed over to the van. She had just opened the sliding side door for Tanner when both of them froze.

Ariana rose from where she had been ducked out of sight in front of the van, even as Brick approached Tanner from behind. The big man had been concealed by the rear of the vehicle.

Tanner saw the threat posed by Ariana, while Alexa had spotted Brick. Tanner was bringing his gun up to shoot Ariana when Brick grabbed him from behind, and as Alexa cocked her arm back to toss a knife at Brick, Ariana placed her gun against the back of Alexa's head.

"I'm Ariana O'Grady, Tanner, and tonight you're going to die."

32

TANNER, MY TANNER

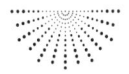

One instant Tanner was bringing the rifle up to shoot Ariana, and the next thing he knew his arms were pinned to his sides and his feet were leaving the ground.

He could only see Brick's massive arms as they began squeezing the life out of him, and he felt the rifle fall from his hands, which were pinned to his sides.

Alexa stood in front of him while holding a knife in a throwing position, but Ariana had a gun pressed to her head. Tanner struggled to break the grip holding him and found that it was useless. Whoever it was that had him, also had twice his strength. If he didn't do something soon, the man would likely crush the life from him.

Tanner kicked at the man, but his feet were finding only thigh. The man had his hip turned so that Tanner's feet wouldn't find his vulnerable crotch.

Tanner moved his head forward and then slammed it backwards, hoping to break the man's nose. Instead, his skull collided with Brick's massive chin. Tanner was stunned from the impact, while the man holding him hadn't even grunted.

When the pain in his right ribs began, it cleared Tanner's head. Brick was squeezing so hard that Tanner's elbow was pressing into his ribs, and he felt as if a rib on the right was about to break from the pressure.

And as the air was crushed from his lungs, Tanner knew he had to do something or die.

~

ALEXA STOOD FROZEN LIKE A STATUE AS SHE WATCHED Tanner struggle in Brick's arms.

After Tanner tried the head butt that failed, she saw that it left him stunned, but then a look of intense pain crossed his face. Alexa moved her hand back farther in preparation to throw her knife at Brick's face, but the woman behind her, the one she could only see peripherally, pressed her weapon harder into the back of Alexa's head. She then called out encouragement to her giant partner.

"That's it, Brick; crush the life out of the murderous bastard. Kill Tanner!"

~

TANNER STRETCHED HIS NECK FORWARD WHILE ALSO bending his left leg upward. When it was close enough, he bit down hard on the shank of wood still stuck in his leg and yanked it free.

The pain in his leg was blinding and competed with the agony in his ribs, but Tanner stayed conscious, reared his head back, then jerked it to the left. The bloody pointed tip of the wood tore into Brick's neck.

Brick's grip disappeared, and Tanner fell to the ground.

∾

Alexa heard Ariana whisper the word, "No," as they both watched Tanner free the jagged splinter from his own leg and use it to spear Brick's throat.

Knowing that Ariana was distracted, Alexa ducked her head, then spun around and grabbed Ariana's gun arm, while trying to get a better grip on the knife in her own hand. She had been holding the knife by its tip in preparation to throw it, but she needed to get a grip on its handle.

Ariana saw what Alexa was doing and grabbed the wrist of the hand holding the knife. The women struggled for a second, then they stumbled backwards into Brick.

Alexa managed to free her hand after the impact. She slashed out at Ariana and cut her face from right to left, ripping her open from lip to brow, even as Ariana and Brick tripped over Tanner, who was still down on one knee.

The slashed and bleeding pair tumbled down the short hill leading to the stream and splashed into it only an instant apart. Ariana let out a scream as Brick bellowed, then the current carried them swiftly out of sight.

∾

Tanner grabbed his rifle from where it had fallen and used it like a crutch to help him stand, as Alexa came to him.

"How badly are you hurt?"

"He nearly broke a rib, but I think my leg is the bigger problem right now."

Alexa looked down at Tanner's leg and saw that it was bleeding freely.

The side door on the van was still sitting open, and she helped him inside. After handing him something to press against the wound, she climbed behind the wheel.

"I'll drive us somewhere else and then treat that leg, or do you think you need a doctor?"

"You do it. If you can't stop the bleeding, we'll try an emergency room."

Alexa drove the van back behind the bowling alley, then went to work treating the wound. She had to clean the wound twice before stitching it closed, but she got the bleeding to stop.

"You've had medical training?" Tanner asked.

"No, but when you've trained with edged weapons as much as I have you learn to treat cuts."

Regardless of that, Alexa could do nothing about Tanner's ribs. After checking to make certain that none had broken, she handed him a bottle of painkiller.

Tanner read the label and frowned. "These will make me drowsy."

"Yes, but they'll also kill the pain. Take them. I'll drive us to the cabin and keep an eye out for any more trouble."

Tanner relented and took the pills. He would likely sleep anyway during the drive to the cabin, because he had barely slept the night before.

"Tanner?"

"Yeah?"

"You tensed up right before that woman and her pet giant attacked us. Why was that, did you sense them at the last moment the way I did?"

Tanner grinned. "No, Alexa, but I did smell Ariana's perfume."

"Oh."

"I guess that sixth sense of yours comes in handy, hmm?"

Alexa smiled. "It helped me to find you."

Tanner fell asleep on an air mattress an hour after taking the medicine, and Alexa drove while occasionally looking back at him in wonder.

A Tanner, no, my Tanner.

There had been an instant while Brick was attempting to crush the life from Tanner that Alexa had believed he would do it, that he would kill Tanner, and that the woman at her back pressing a gun against her head would pull the trigger and kill her.

But then, Alexa had looked at Tanner's face. She glimpsed pain there, but no panic or even a trace of fear. Tanner then turned the tables by never giving up and using his mind to find a way to win. That was the legend she had heard growing up.

Rodrigo had always spoken of his Tanner, Tanner Five, as if he were more than a man, and she had thrilled when he told her stories about the things he had seen the man do. Those stories had inspired her in her quest to kill Alonso Alvarado, although deep in her heart, she knew there lurked doubt that she would ever be able to do it.

Alvarado lived in a virtual fortress, was protected by a personal army, and had the wealth and resources to survive any attack and vanquish any foe.

Alexa grinned. *Almost* any foe.

Alvarado would not survive this Tanner, her Tanner, and together she and Tanner would have their revenge.

She gazed back at Tanner's sleeping form once more while stopped at a traffic light. He was injured, but he would heal soon, then they would travel to Mexico and kill Alvarado. And after that?

Alexa smiled. After that would come pleasure, there would be peace, and perhaps, just perhaps, there might be love.

Alexa drove on into the night toward the cabin. For the first time in many months, her thoughts were about something other than gaining revenge.

33
TWO

Amy breathed a sigh of relief when she heard the shower turn on.

She had spent the last few hours covertly looking around the cabin for the drawing of Alexa she'd had earlier. After she couldn't find it anywhere, she realized she must have left it inside the other cabin.

She thought about telling Spenser about her mistake, but he was wary enough about bringing her along. If she admitted to leaving the flyer behind after they searched the cabin, he might insist that she head back to Wyoming.

She chastised herself again for having been so careless, and as Spenser took his shower, she snuck out the front door and headed over to the cabin Alexa had rented. Amy knew she had to hurry, because Tanner and Alexa could come at any time, and Spenser wouldn't be in the shower forever.

She entered the cabin through the unlocked rear door and used her phone like a flashlight to look around. She had been searching for over a minute and was becoming frustrated when she remembered where she must have left the flyer. Amy entered the bedroom, opened the closet door, and jumped when the closet light came on automatically.

~

Alexa stopped the van out on the road and was blocking the lane that led to the three cabins. She had seen a light come on in their cabin and knew that someone was lurking around inside. Alexa cut off the headlights, moved the van very slowly, and reached for a knife.

~

Amy smiled as she spotted the flyer sitting on the closet shelf. She had laid it there when she went through the duffel bag that Alexa had left on the closet floor, then had forgotten to take it with her.

She closed the door, and then once again, she used her phone to navigate the darkness. She left by the back door, moved toward the front of her own cabin, and saw Alexa's van.

Amy panicked and ran for her front door as Alexa slammed on her brakes.

~

Alexa threw the van in park and called out, "Tanner, wake up!" She didn't wait to see if he'd heard her, she had her eyes on Amy.

Amy was inside her own cabin and closing the door when Alexa smashed into it, causing Amy to scream as she fell backwards.

Alexa was on her in an instant, and Amy struggled

until Alexa placed a knife to her throat while holding her from behind. She was about to ask her who else was in the cabin when a bearded man wearing only an eye patch and a towel came from a room down the short hallway.

Other than the eye patch and the towel, Alexa noticed two other things about the man. He was in superb condition, and he was holding a gun and pointing it right at her.

The man had just walked past the open doorway when Tanner appeared. Alexa felt Amy inhale to speak, to warn the one-eyed man, and she clamped a hand over her mouth to stifle her words.

~

Spenser had just dried himself off and was wrapping a towel around his waist when he heard Amy scream. He scooped his gun off the bedside table and found that Alexa and Amy were on the floor in the living room, and that Alexa was threatening Amy with a knife.

When Amy opened her mouth to speak, Alexa clamped a hand over her lips, but then Amy's eyes grew large with alarm as she stared at something behind him.

Spenser realized that Amy was trying to warn him. This thought was instantly confirmed when Amy kicked her foot out to change the angle on the flat-screen TV, and with his good eye, Spenser saw Tanner reflected in its blank surface.

~

Alexa watched Tanner enter the room and wondered just how drowsy the pain pills had made him. He was limping into the cabin but had kept his gun in the holster on his belt. She was about to shout to him to defend himself, but she was too late, and the man with the eye patch turned toward him swiftly. However, even as the man did so, he lowered his gun. Then, to Alexa's shock, Tanner and the man shook hands warmly amid huge grins.

∼

Tanner raised up a hand and spoke to Alexa. "Let her go. She's on our side."

Alexa blinked rapidly. "What?"

"It's all right, Alexa; they're friends."

Alexa released Amy and the two women got to their feet. Spenser took Amy by the hand and pulled her over to be near him.

"What happened, Amy?"

Amy pointed to the drawing of Alexa. It had fallen to the floor while they had struggled.

"I left that in their cabin when we were there earlier, and while you were showering... I snuck back in to get it. When she saw me coming out, I panicked and ran, and she ran after me."

Alexa walked over to Tanner. "What's going on?"

"As I said, they're friends of mine, or at least Spenser is, this is the first time I'm meeting Amy, although I've heard good things about her."

"Why didn't you tell me that you knew these people?" Alexa said.

"I trusted you, Alexa, but I had to be sure. Spenser followed you from Oklahoma City to here, and then from here back to Oklahoma City. If you weren't who and what you said you were, that would have been an ideal time to contact someone. When Spenser told me that you made no stops other than for gas and groceries, it confirmed what I believed, that I could trust you."

Alexa's face screwed up in confusion. "You had someone follow me? But no, I would have seen him."

Tanner shook his head. "Not Spenser you wouldn't; he's too good to allow himself to be spotted."

Alexa sucked in a breath as a pained expression darkened her face. "I thought you trusted me when you sent me here, but you were just testing me? Goddamn it, Tanner, what do I have to do to prove myself to you? Should I let Alvarado kill me, would that convince you?"

Alexa rushed out the open doorway and back to her van. After parking it in front of their cabin, she just sat inside it.

One tear escaped, then two, she wiped them away in anger as Tanner limped over toward her.

When she looked at him, he sent her a shrug.

"I won't apologize for testing you, but I do want you to know that I trust you completely now."

Alexa reached out the window, gave him a weak slap across the face, and called him several unflattering names in Spanish.

"Are you through now? Because if you are, I want you to come inside and see Spenser."

Alexa smirked. "If that towel had slipped any lower, I would have seen all of Spenser." She stepped from the van and looked Tanner over. "How do you feel? Do you need to see a doctor?"

"The leg hurts some, but the ribs are worse. Still, I'll heal, and we need time to plan our attack on Alvarado in any event. Spenser convinced me that if I rushed into Mexico without a plan, I might never get out alive."

"Your friend is right, and we'll plan while your ribs

heal, but one way or another, I will see that bastard Alvarado dead."

They returned to Spenser's cabin and found that Spenser had dressed. He was wearing boots, jeans, and a green short sleeve sweatshirt.

Alexa found him to be handsome and thought that the eye patch gave him a mysterious air. When Amy walked up to her and extended her hand, Alexa shook it, then smiled.

"I didn't like going through your things, Alexa," Amy said. "But Spenser thought it was necessary."

"I was angry before, but I understand your need to be certain about me," Alexa told Amy, and then she spoke to Tanner. "Will Spenser and Amy be coming with us when we go to see Tanner Six?"

Tanner smiled. "Alexa, Spenser Hawke *is* Tanner Six."

Alexa stared at Spenser, and then back at Tanner. When she looked over at Amy, Amy just shrugged.

Alexa gave a little laugh. "Tanner Six, oh Spenser, you've got to meet my Papa, he would love to talk to you. He knew Tanner Five."

Spenser studied Alexa. "Your last name is Lucia?"

"It is now, because I took the name of the man who raised me, but I was born Alexa Cazares."

"The man who raised you, is he Rodrigo Lucia?"

"Yes. Do you know him?"

"Tanner Five mentioned him on occasion, I think he was happiest when he lived with Rodrigo's mother and traveled with their circus, he said he even did an act as a trick shooter while he was with them."

"Yes, Papa mentioned that," Alexa said.

Spenser looked over at Tanner. "How did you get injured, was it the men I warned you about?"

"Yes and no, I injured the leg while avoiding a grenade

blast by one of the men sent to kill me, but the ribs were caused by a brute working for someone else."

"I assumed this brute and his keeper were handled?"

"For now. If they pop up again, they'll wish they hadn't."

Spenser laid a hand on Tanner's shoulder. "It's so damn good to see you, boy, and I've missed you."

Tanner smiled. "I've missed you too, old man."

"Old?" Amy said. "Spenser's only in his forties."

"It's a sort of joke," Spenser said. "Tanner and I have a father and son vibe going, and someday, Amy, I want you to meet my other boy, Romeo."

"I saw him and Nadya recently," Tanner said. "He told me that they'll be here next year… after the baby is born."

Spenser grinned. "Yeah, he told me about that."

Amy laughed. "That means I'll soon be dating a grandfather."

∽

Tanner and Alexa said goodnight and entered their cabin.

Alexa pointed at the sofa. "I should make you sleep on that for taking so long to trust me, but since you're injured I'll show mercy and let you share the bed with me."

"You're very kind," Tanner said, and kissed her. When the kissing grew more passionate, Alexa broke off from Tanner and headed for the bedroom.

"I need a shower, but you shower first, and then I'll place a better bandage on that leg wound."

Tanner followed and leaned in the bedroom doorway. "Alexa."

She had been unpacking her duffel bag, but she turned and looked at him.

"Yes?"

"I don't really understand how you found me, but I'm glad you did."

Alexa smiled brightly at him. "I'm here and I'm staying."

They kissed once more, then Tanner limped into the bathroom.

34

WHAT THING?

At St. Anthony's Hospital in Oklahoma City, Nurse Marion Brown had just finished thinking about what a quiet night it had been so far. That was when the giant American Indian walked in with what looked like a stick jutting from his neck.

The man's clothes were damp, although it wasn't raining, and he carried an unconscious woman in his arms who had a nasty cut on her face.

Marion called for an orderly to bring over a stretcher, then watched as the Indian laid the woman gently upon it.

"Oh my God, sir, what happened to you two?"

Brick smiled. "It's just a mild case of Tanneritis."

A second orderly brought over a wheelchair, but when Brick tried to sit his massive frame down into it, the handles became wedged around his hips. He pushed the chair aside and spoke to Nurse Marion.

"I'll walk; it's good exercise."

"Yes," Marion said. "And then we'll have a doctor remove that thing in your neck."

Brick gave her a perplexed look. "What thing in my neck?"

Marion looked unsure how to respond to that, and Brick let out a loud laugh before he followed along behind Ariana's stretcher.

∾

Tanner came out of the bathroom after showering and sat on the side of the bed. He was only wearing a pair of black boxers, and Alexa got down on her knees between his legs.

Tanner smiled at her. "I thought we might kiss first, but I'm not complaining."

Alexa laughed as she reached over to the nightstand and grabbed the sterilized gauze and antiseptic cream.

"I'm down here to place a fresh bandage on your leg."

"I see," Tanner said.

Alexa bandaged the wound in his left leg and then stood, leaned over, and kissed him.

"I'm going to take a long hot shower, so you might as well go to sleep."

Tanner's eyes flicked to the gap in her blouse. The view pleased him.

"I think I'll stay awake and see what develops."

Alexa ran a hand through his hair. "You need rest, and… certain strenuous activities might aggravate your rib injury."

Tanner kissed her. "Go take that shower."

Alexa did so, and when she left the bathroom, she was wearing a long baseball jersey with the team's name written across it, The Mexico City Red Devils, Los Diablos Rojos del Mexico.

The shirt was red with white lettering, and it fell to

mid-thigh on her. Tanner took in Alexa's long, sexy legs, and when he met her eyes, he saw that she was smiling.

Alexa turned out the light and crawled into bed beside him.

"I didn't pack a nightgown, but I think I'll go shopping for some soon."

"The shorter the better," Tanner said.

Alexa snuggled against him, but gently. Tanner had a wounded leg on one side, and sore ribs on the other.

"Are we really safe here?" Alexa asked.

"Yes, but Spenser will set up perimeter alarms anyway."

"Does he live in the area?"

"No, Spenser lives in Wyoming." Tanner brushed Alexa's hair from her eyes and kissed her. "When you took my hand the other day, you said the words, 'Cody' and 'buffalo.'"

"Yes?"

"Spenser's home, it's in Cody, Wyoming, and it was named after a man named Buffalo Bill Cody."

"Ah, and that's why you were so upset? You thought I knew where to find Tanner Six, and there was no way for me to know that."

They were quiet for a few moments, just laying together in the dark, but then, Tanner broke the silence.

"The name Cody, it's also my real name. I'm Cody Parker, and uh, Martillo, that bastard Alonso Alvarado, he slaughtered my family the same way he killed yours."

Alexa sat up, put on the light, and stared at Tanner. "Oh my God, how old were you?"

"I was grown, mostly grown, I was sixteen. If not for Spenser, I would have died that day. He's also the man who crippled Alvarado years ago."

"Why didn't he kill him?"

"He thought he had, and believed it for nearly twenty years, but the son of a bitch survived somehow... just like I did."

"And as I did as well," Alexa said.

She turned off the light and laid back down beside Tanner, to rest her head on his chest.

"We both owe that monster so much, and soon we will make him pay."

"Yes."

"Tanner, who did you lose?"

"My two sisters, my father, stepmother, and my baby brother."

"What were their names?"

Tanner sighed. "It doesn't matter."

Alexa kissed him gently upon the lips. "It does matter, because they are the ones you'll be killing this monster for, just as I will avenge my family."

Tanner began to talk, telling Alexa stories about his family, about his twin sisters, and as he talked, he recalled things about them all that he had nearly forgotten. When he finished, they faded off to sleep, fellow victims of the past, who would soon make their tormentor pay.

35
3 PLUS 1 EQUALS 4

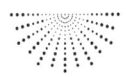

When Scar realized that the large black crows had been devouring parts of Steve Bennett, he upchucked the Egg McMuffin he'd eaten only minutes earlier.

Scar, Bruise, Wound, and Abrasion woke early and went looking for Steve Bennett and the other strike team members after Bennett didn't answer his phone. When they decided to go to where they last saw the strike team, they came across their vehicle parked at the entrance to the house.

Scar tried calling the number again as he pulled his motorcycle up to the front of the demolished house and heard the phone ringing nearby. He and the other Horsemen walked toward the field and found the crows and the bodies.

Abrasion looked around. "Where's the black guy, Hakeem?"

Wound pointed out toward the old shack, where over a dozen more crows were feasting.

"I bet that's him."

The phone had stopped ringing, but it started right

back up. Scar plucked the phone from a pile of goo he hoped was just mud and answered the call while placing it in speaker mode.

A man's voice came out of the device loud and clear. It was Robert Martinez of Hexalcorp; he was calling Bennett for an update at Alonso Alvarado's insistence.

"Steve? Thank God, why weren't any of you answering your phones?"

"Bennett's dead," Scar said, and heard a noise that sounded like a whimper on the other end of the line.

"Oh my God. Who am I talking to? Tanner, is that you?"

"My name is Scar. Me and my gang were doing some work for Bennett and his boys, but they're all dead now."

"All of them?"

"Yeah, I think they were mostly shot up, but Bennett looks like he swallowed a bomb, he's all in pieces. I'm amazed this phone works."

The line grew quiet as Martinez tried to think of some way to salvage things. If he didn't do something, Alvarado would murder him.

"What's your name again?"

"Scar."

"Scar? Oh wait, you're the guys that spotted the woman at that motel Tanner was at, right?"

"That's us, and if we ever see her again we'll make her damn sorry she ever messed with us."

"You and your gang, there are four of you, correct?"

Scar took a head count. Came up with three, but then remembered to count himself too.

"Yeah, there are four of us, why?"

"Never mind, just listen to what I say. If you follow my instructions, I'll make you and your friends rich."

"You're talking about Tanner?"

"Yes, but I'll give you each ten grand even if you never find Tanner."

"Say that again."

"You heard me right. My name is Martinez and I'll pay you ten grand each, five now and five later, but you have to do exactly as I tell you."

Scar looked at Wound, Bruise, and Abrasion, and saw that all three of them were nodding their heads.

"All right, Mr. Martinez, tell us what to do."

∾

Six hours later, the Hexalcorp Strike Team was back on the hunt.

Martinez instructed Scar and the other Tin Horsemen to strip Bennett and his men of all ID and weapons and then to bury the bodies. They were to take on the men's identities and have the use of their vehicle and credit cards.

Bennett and his men might be dead, but Martinez did not intend to follow them into the hereafter. If he could keep the truth from Alvarado until Tanner was either killed or believed to be in hiding, he just might make it out of this mess alive.

∾

The new Hexalcorp Strike Team, the former Tin Horsemen, were tooling along the highway in Bennett's huge pickup truck after paying a local gas station to store their bikes. They were all five grand richer thanks to Martinez, with a shot of getting five thousand more.

Scar laughed as he drove. "This is a sweet ride and look at all the weapons we've got. Hell, I bet we could kill Tanner, why not?"

Abrasion was sitting in the back holding Hakeem's rifle. He had also taken the man's name, while Wound was now Wilson, and Bruise was Simms.

Abrasion stroked Hakeem's rifle as if he was its lover. "Get me close to Tanner with this baby and I'll blast him to pieces, homie."

Scar looked into the rearview mirror. "Homie?"

"Hakeem was black, right?"

"Yeah, but dude, he didn't talk like that. Don't be a racist."

Abrasion ducked his head. "Sorry, and I didn't mean anything by it. I thought Hakeem was cool; it's why I took his name."

Bennett's phone rang, and Scar placed it on speakerphone. "Bennett here, Chief."

Martinez' sigh filled the car. "It's good that you're using his name, but don't call me chief."

"Okay, but what's up?"

"Tanner seems to be in the wind, but I've got a lead on the other man we're looking for. There's a guy up in Wyoming that swears he used to sell him fuel."

"So, you want us to go to a gas station in Wyoming?"

"No, it's diesel fuel for a generator, and the guy knows where he lives."

"We'll check it out."

"I've sent the address to that phone, and don't get too excited; I think the lead is a dud."

"Why do you say that?"

There was static on the line, but then Martinez came back on. "What did you say, Scar? I couldn't hear you."

"I asked why you thought this tip was a dud."

"Oh, the guy you're going to check out, he only has one eye. Call me when you get there, Martinez out."

36

ONE TANNER, TWO TANNI?

Tanner's leg felt better when he woke, but his ribs still ached from Brick's attack.

Alexa had risen before him, had showered again, and was wearing a different T-shirt. It was one of Tanner's. It hung on her like a short black dress.

"Good morning," she said, and then she kissed him.

"Is that coffee I smell?"

"It is, and how are you feeling?"

"Not bad, except for the ribs."

Tanner grabbed a fresh pair of boxers and headed for the shower. When he came out, he sat on the side of the bed.

Alexa had been sitting in a chair watching the news. She shut off the TV, walked over to the bed, and lowered herself between Tanner's legs.

Tanner gave his bandaged leg a good look.

"I don't think that dressing needs changing yet."

Alexa smiled as she removed the T-shirt she was wearing.

"I agree with you."

~

When they finally emerged from their cabin in the early afternoon, Tanner and Alexa found Spenser coming back from a walk around the lake.

He smiled at them. "You two looked rested."

"We are," Tanner said.

Spenser was standing by his truck; he leaned back against it. "Alexa, tell me more about Rodrigo."

Tanner pointed toward Spenser's cabin. "I think I should talk to Amy."

"Do that, and Alexa and I will have a chat at the same time."

"She knows, Spenser. She knows that my real name is Cody Parker."

Spenser raised an eyebrow. "I see, and Amy knows as well."

Tanner looked surprised at that, and perhaps a little perturbed by it as well.

Spenser saw his reaction and shrugged. "I love her, son, and I promised her that there would be no more secrets between us. I trust her and you can too."

Tanner went inside and found Amy in the kitchen. She was seated at the breakfast nook, which offered a view of the lake.

She sent Tanner a tentative smile. "How are you doing?"

"I'm healing, and I've come to thank you for helping Spenser."

"I love him, Tanner."

Tanner settled himself in a chair across the table from Amy. "You can call me Cody. I always feel a little odd being called Tanner when I'm around Spenser, since he's a Tanner too."

"He doesn't do that anymore, take contracts."

"Doesn't he? Isn't that what he does when he's helping his clients?"

Amy thought that over and nodded. "I guess that's true, but those people are desperate and have nowhere else to turn when they seek him out, and he does a lot of good."

"Yes, he does, and I hear that you help him sometimes too."

Amy smiled, and then laughed.

"Did I say something funny?"

"No, it's just that, well, when Spenser first showed me that wanted poster of you and I read about what a violent and deadly man you were… it's… I'll just say you're not what I expected. And I can tell that you and Spenser love each other."

Tanner grabbed the carafe that was sitting on the table and poured himself a cup of coffee.

"We're family, Spenser and I, and if I'm reading him right, you may soon be joining that family."

"He hasn't asked me to marry him, but yes, I think that's where we're headed. But first, first Spenser has to help you deal with what's in Mexico."

Tanner stopped his cup halfway to his lips and stared at Amy. "What's this about Mexico? Spenser's not going down there with me."

Amy nodded, as concern lit her face. "Yes, he is, and I'm so worried for him."

∼

When Tanner came out of the cabin with Amy following behind, he found Spenser and Alexa laughing together over something, as they spoke in Spanish.

He marched up to Spenser. "You're not coming to Mexico. That's not what this was about. I came to see you to pick your brain, not to ask you to risk your life."

Spenser had been leaning back against his truck; he straightened up and placed a hand on Tanner's shoulder.

"This isn't all about you. I failed, Cody. I had that bastard Alvarado broken in pieces and left for dead, but somehow, damn it, somehow that son of a bitch made it out of that burning house and has been living his monstrous life all these years. That's my fault, son, my failure, and not you or anyone else is going to stop me from finally seeing him dead."

Tanner removed Spenser's hand from his shoulder. "No. It's too dangerous, because of your missing eye. It's why you passed the Tanner name to me when you were still so young."

"I passed the name on because you were ready. Hell, Cody, I risk my life all the time because that's how I live. I feed on the challenge, even the danger, and I'll tell you right now, I'm as good as I ever was."

Tanner shook his head in disagreement, then he did something that truly hurt him to do. He threw a punch at Spenser, a right hook aimed at Spenser's blind side.

Spenser blocked the punch by grabbing Tanner's wrist.

"What was that, a test? Try that again, boy, and I'll knock you on your ass."

Tanner lowered his hand as he chuckled. "Yes, sir, but how the hell did you see that punch coming?"

Spenser pointed at the side-view mirror on Alexa's van. "I've learned to compensate for the injury over the years. I had to, because I refuse to live my life at half speed."

Tanner raised his hand again, but this time it was to offer to shake with Spenser.

Spenser gripped Tanner's hand and smiled. "We're

going down to Mexico, Cody, and we're going to finally put that monster Alvarado in the ground."

This time, Alexa held up a hand. She did so to clarify something.

"Am I hearing this right? Both of you will be helping me to kill Alvarado?"

"That's right," the two men said at the same time.

Alexa smiled, then she laughed. As she went to Tanner, he placed an arm around her waist.

"Two Tanners. Oh, Alonso Alvarado and his cartel are doomed."

Spenser took Amy's hand, kissed it, and then he tousled Tanner's hair playfully.

"Not only are they doomed, Alexa, but I know exactly how we're going to do it."

TANNER RETURNS!

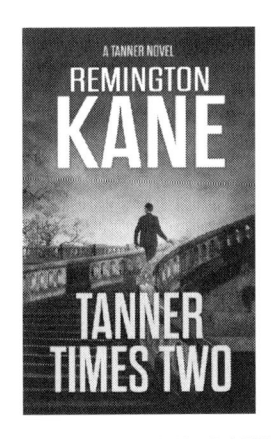

TANNER TIMES TWO - BOOK 11

AFTERWORD

Thank you,

REMINGTON KANE

JOIN MY INNER CIRCLE

You'll receive FREE books, such as,

SLAY BELLS – A TANNER NOVEL – BOOK 0

TAKEN! ALPHABET SERIES – 26 ORIGINAL TAKEN! TALES

BLUE STEELE - KARMA

Also – Exclusive short stories featuring TANNER, along with other books.

TO BECOME AN INNER CIRCLE MEMBER, GO TO:
http://remingtonkane.com/mailing-list/

ALSO BY REMINGTON KANE

The TANNER Series in order

INEVITABLE I - A Tanner Novel - Book 1

KILL IN PLAIN SIGHT - A Tanner Novel - Book 2

MAKING A KILLING ON WALL STREET - A Tanner Novel - Book 3

THE FIRST ONE TO DIE LOSES - A Tanner Novel - Book 4

THE LIFE & DEATH OF CODY PARKER - A Tanner Novel - Book 5

WAR - A Tanner Novel- A Tanner Novel - Book 6

SUICIDE OR DEATH - A Tanner Novel - Book 7

TWO FOR THE KILL - A Tanner Novel - Book 8

BALLET OF DEATH - A Tanner Novel - Book 9

MORE DANGEROUS THAN MAN - A Tanner Novel - Book 10

TANNER TIMES TWO - A Tanner Novel - Book 11

OCCUPATION: DEATH - A Tanner Novel - Book 12

HELL FOR HIRE - A Tanner Novel - Book 13

A HOME TO DIE FOR - A Tanner Novel - Book 14

FIRE WITH FIRE - A Tanner Novel - Book 15

TO KILL A KILLER - A Tanner Novel - Book 16

WHITE HELL – A Tanner Novel - Book 17

MANHATTAN HIT MAN – A Tanner Novel - Book 18

ONE HUNDRED YEARS OF TANNER – A Tanner Novel -

Book 19

REVELATIONS - A Tanner Novel - Book 20

THE SPY GAME - A Tanner Novel - Book 21

A VICTIM OF CIRCUMSTANCE - A Tanner Novel - Book 22

A MAN OF RESPECT - A Tanner Novel - Book 23

THE MAN, THE MYTH - A Tanner Novel - Book 24

ALL-OUT WAR - A Tanner Novel - Book 25

THE REAL DEAL - A Tanner Novel - Book 26

WAR ZONE - A Tanner Novel - Book 27

ULTIMATE ASSASSIN - A Tanner Novel - Book 28

KNIGHT TIME - A Tanner Novel - Book 29

PROTECTOR - A Tanner Novel - Book 30

BULLETS BEFORE BREAKFAST - A Tanner Novel - Book 31

VENGEANCE - A Tanner Novel - Book 32

TARGET: TANNER - A Tanner Novel - Book 33

BLACK SHEEP - A Tanner Novel - Book 34

FLESH AND BLOOD - A Tanner Novel - Book 35

NEVER SEE IT COMING - A Tanner Novel - Book 36

MISSING - A Tanner Novel - Book 37

CONTENDER - A Tanner Novel - Book 38

TO SERVE AND PROTECT - A Tanner Novel - Book 39

STALKING HORSE - A Tanner Novel - Book 40

THE EVIL OF TWO LESSERS - A Tanner Novel - Book 41

SINS OF THE FATHER AND MOTHER - A Tanner Novel - Book 42

SOULLESS - A Tanner Novel - Book 43

The Young Guns Series in order

YOUNG GUNS

YOUNG GUNS 2 - SMOKE & MIRRORS

YOUNG GUNS 3 - BEYOND LIMITS

YOUNG GUNS 4 - RYKER'S RAIDERS

YOUNG GUNS 5 - ULTIMATE TRAINING

YOUNG GUNS 6 - CONTRACT TO KILL

YOUNG GUNS 7 - FIRST LOVE

YOUNG GUNS 8 - THE END OF THE BEGINNING

A Tanner Series in order

TANNER: YEAR ONE

TANNER: YEAR TWO

TANNER: YEAR THREE

TANNER: YEAR FOUR

TANNER: YEAR FIVE

The TAKEN! Series in order

TAKEN! - LOVE CONQUERS ALL - Book 1

TAKEN! - SECRETS & LIES - Book 2

TAKEN! - STALKER - Book 3

TAKEN! - BREAKOUT! - Book 4

TAKEN! - THE THIRTY-NINE - Book 5

TAKEN! - KIDNAPPING THE DEVIL - Book 6

TAKEN! - HIT SQUAD - Book 7

TAKEN! - MASQUERADE - Book 8

TAKEN! - SERIOUS BUSINESS - Book 9

TAKEN! - THE COUPLE THAT SLAYS TOGETHER - Book 10

TAKEN! - PUT ASUNDER - Book 11

TAKEN! - LIKE BOND, ONLY BETTER - Book 12

TAKEN! - MEDIEVAL - Book 13

TAKEN! - RISEN! - Book 14

TAKEN! - VACATION - Book 15

TAKEN! - MICHAEL - Book 16

TAKEN! - BEDEVILED - Book 17

TAKEN! - INTENTIONAL ACTS OF VIOLENCE - Book 18

TAKEN! - THE KING OF KILLERS – Book 19

TAKEN! - NO MORE MR. NICE GUY - Book 20 & the Series Finale

The MR. WHITE Series

PAST IMPERFECT - MR. WHITE - Book 1

HUNTED - MR. WHITE - Book 2

The BLUE STEELE Series in order

BLUE STEELE - BOUNTY HUNTER- Book 1

BLUE STEELE - BROKEN- Book 2

BLUE STEELE - VENGEANCE- Book 3

BLUE STEELE - THAT WHICH DOESN'T KILL ME- Book 4

BLUE STEELE - ON THE HUNT- Book 5

BLUE STEELE - PAST SINS - Book 6

BLUE STEELE - DADDY'S GIRL - Book 7 & the Series Finale

The CALIBER DETECTIVE AGENCY Series in order

CALIBER DETECTIVE AGENCY - GENERATIONS- Book 1

CALIBER DETECTIVE AGENCY - TEMPTATION- Book 2

CALIBER DETECTIVE AGENCY - A RANSOM PAID IN BLOOD- Book 3

CALIBER DETECTIVE AGENCY - MISSING- Book 4

CALIBER DETECTIVE AGENCY - DECEPTION- Book 5

CALIBER DETECTIVE AGENCY - CRUCIBLE- Book 6

CALIBER DETECTIVE AGENCY – LEGENDARY – Book 7

CALIBER DETECTIVE AGENCY – WE ARE GATHERED HERE TODAY - Book 8

CALIBER DETECTIVE AGENCY - MEANS, MOTIVE, and OPPORTUNITY - Book 9 & the Series Finale

THE TAKEN!/TANNER Series in order

THE CONTRACT: KILL JESSICA WHITE - Taken!/Tanner - Book 1

UNFINISHED BUSINESS – Taken!/Tanner – Book 2

THE ABDUCTION OF THOMAS LAWSON - Taken!/Tanner – Book 3

PREDATOR - Taken!/Tanner - Book 4

DETECTIVE PIERCE Series in order

MONSTERS - A Detective Pierce Novel - Book 1

DEMONS - A Detective Pierce Novel - Book 2

ANGELS - A Detective Pierce Novel - Book 3

THE OCEAN BEACH ISLAND Series in order

THE MANY AND THE ONE - Book 1

SINS & SECOND CHANES - Book 2

DRY ADULTERY, WET AMBITION - Book 3

OF TONGUE AND PEN - Book 4

ALL GOOD THINGS… - Book 5

LITTLE WHITE SINS - Book 6

THE LIGHT OF DARKNESS - Book 7

STERN ISLAND - Book 8 & the Series Finale

THE REVENGE Series in order

JOHNNY REVENGE - The Revenge Series - Book 1

THE APPOINTMENT KILLER - The Revenge Series - Book 2

AN I FOR AN I - The Revenge Series - Book 3

ALSO

THE EFFECT: Reality is changing!

THE FIX-IT MAN: A Tale of True Love and Revenge

DOUBLE OR NOTHING

PARKER & KNIGHT

REDEMPTION: Someone's taken her

DESOLATION LAKE

TIME TRAVEL TALES & OTHER SHORT STORIES

MORE DANGEROUS THAN MAN
Copyright © REMINGTON KANE, 2015
YEAR ZERO PUBLISHING, LLC

This book is a work of fiction. Names, characters, places and incidents either are products of the author's imagination or are used fictitiously.

Any resemblance to actual events or locales or persons, living or dead, is entirely coincidental.

All rights reserved. Except as permitted under the U.S. Copyright Act of 1976, no part of this publication may be reproduced, distributed or transmitted in any form or by any means, or stored in a database or retrieval system, without the prior written permission of the publisher.

❦ Created with Vellum

Printed in Great Britain
by Amazon